UNDISCOVERED
AFFINITY

By the Author

Capturing Jessica

Undiscovered Affinity

UNDISCOVERED AFFINITY

by
Jane Hardee

2018

UNDISCOVERED AFFINITY

ISBN 13: 978-1-63555-061-0

This Trade Paperback Original Is Published By
Bold Strokes Books, Inc.
P.O. Box 249
Valley Falls, NY 12185

First Edition: February 2018

Credits
Editor: Cindy Cresap
Production Design: Stacia Seaman
Cover Art by Mr
Cover Design by Melody Pond

Acknowledgments

A huge thank you to Bold Strokes Books for considering and publishing my work. Thanks to Cindy Cresap, Sandy Lowe, and all the BSB staff for their support and wealth of knowledge about what I consider a very daunting process.

Endless thanks to my editor, Katia Noyes, for her expertise, sense of humor, and tolerance. One of these days I will understand Microsoft Word, Katia, I promise.

A special thanks to all those plus-size beauties out there. The ones who wear bikinis and the ones who don't. The ones who take nude selfies and the ones who cover their bellies when someone takes a picture. The ones who know through and through that they are amazing and the ones who need reminding. Please know that the only standard of beauty you need to meet is your own.

And of course, thanks to the readers. I hope you enjoy reading this story as much as I enjoyed writing it.

To Lele. I love you bigger than my heart.

CHAPTER ONE

The cool air of the plane cabin was a welcome change from the humid, heavy air of the Amazon jungle. Cardic used to think plane seats were small and uncomfortable, but after eighteen months sitting on the ground or in a poorly made hammock, this coach seat felt like a throne. The plush cushion felt almost uncomfortable.

As the seat belt light chimed, Cardic stuffed the novel she had bought at the Rio de Janeiro-Galeao International Airport back into her messenger bag and adjusted the air vent to blow more forcefully. She ran a hand through her hair as it tickled her forehead, realizing it had gotten much too long. Top on her list of first-world comforts would be a night in her own bed, but a close second was a haircut. Cardic buckled her seat belt and craned her neck to see if the flirty flight attendant was still eyeing her. The second they made eye contact, the flight attendant, who had introduced herself as Iris, came sauntering toward her.

"Pardon me, Dr. Lawson, but if you need to use the lavatory, now is the time," Iris whispered close to her ear, her breast brushing Cardic's shoulder.

Cardic touched Iris's wrist. It was a late flight from Brazil, and most of the other passengers seemed to be asleep, or at the very least not paying attention. "Iris, the seat belt light is illuminated. Do you think I could make it quick?" Cardic grinned and licked her lips again.

"I think the lavatory to the left in the rear of the cabin is vacant. Would you like me to go check for you?"

Unbelievable. Cardic thought it would be at least three days before she found the time or energy to put into sex, but here she was, about to join the Mile High Club and she hadn't even touched down on American soil yet. She was thankful she'd spent the night in a semi-nice hotel and taken a real shower the night before. The pounding of the hot water on her muscles beat bathing in a stream and drying her body with moss.

"Yes, thank you, Iris. I'll be right behind you."

As a ripple of arousal made its way through her body, Cardic waited for a few beats before standing and stretching her arms. She glanced around discreetly to make sure no one was paying her any mind, then she headed toward the lavatory.

After knocking on the left door, she was greeted with a sexy smile as she squeezed her large frame into the cramped space. Iris's perfume was flowery and a little too spicy, but Cardic was already throbbing with anticipation at touching another woman. The logical part of her brain tried to figure out how the hell they were supposed to fuck in this shoe box, then biology and instinct took over.

With her arms braced on the small sink, Cardic dipped her head to taste the smooth skin on Iris's neck. Iris pulled at Cardic's polo and ran her hands underneath to stroke her stomach. Cardic felt a moment of pride at Iris's intake of breath as her fingers met firm muscles. During her time with the Yanapo tribe, her body reached a level of fitness she had never been able to achieve in the gym.

Cardic ground her pelvis into Iris, not trying to hide her

desperation. Her time in the jungle had been her longest stint of abstinence since she started having sex at sixteen. She also didn't care what Iris thought since she knew she'd likely never see her again.

Iris purred in her ear and grabbed the long hair at the nape of her neck. "I've never done this before. But God, you're so sexy. I couldn't let you get away." Iris dipped her hand below Cardic's waistband just above her fly and ran her finger back and forth over the sensitive skin there.

Cardic exhaled through her nose and tensed her muscles. She unbuttoned Iris's starched flight attendant shirt, thankful she'd bought the ninety-nine-cent nail clippers at the hotel gift shop.

"Not all the way, there's no time," Iris said as she grabbed Cardic's wrist and pushed it down toward the hem of her skirt. Cardic dipped her head to taste the skin between Iris's breasts and almost cursed as her backside hit the other side of the lavatory with a loud thud.

Iris's breasts jiggled with her laughter, and Cardic pinched one hard nipple to keep Iris from laughing out loud. "Quiet, or I won't get to make you come."

"Oh, please don't stop." Iris pushed her breasts more firmly toward Cardic's mouth as Cardic pushed her silk panties aside. Finding Iris wet and open, she pushed inside and pumped her hand. Though she was usually one to take her time and map out all the intricacies of a woman's flesh, she urged herself on, knowing the sooner Iris came, the sooner she could have those plump pink lips around her own clit. She wasn't in the mood for a hand job, so somehow she had to make this work.

"Yes, yes." Iris's head fell back against the small mirror. Her muscles clutched at Cardic's fingers and her arms went limp at her sides as she bit her lip to keep quiet. *Well, that was easy.* Either someone wasn't doing their job, or Iris had gone as long as Cardic had without sex. Somehow Cardic thought it was the former.

"My turn," she whispered, withdrawing her fingers and putting them in her mouth. As Iris unbuckled the belt on her khakis, Cardic glanced around the small space. She pushed her pants down to her knees, placed one foot next to the toilet, then the other, and faced Iris. Her neck was in an awkward position, and the side of her head smashed against the ceiling of the cramped space, but all she could think about was coming in Iris's mouth.

Iris pulled her khakis the rest of the way down, and half bent, half knelt in front of Cardic. The girl must have strong calves. All thought left Cardic's mind as she felt the first gentle swipe of Iris's tongue. *Oh my God.* It had been so long. She wasn't going to last. Every ounce of blood rushed to her groin as her mouth dropped open, and she squeezed her eyes shut, wanting to make this last at least a few seconds.

As Iris brought her fingers into play, Cardic grabbed at the back of Iris's head, careful not to disturb the fluffy bun at the top. She didn't want to send her back out there with sex hair. She was at work, after all. Cardic pushed herself as close to Iris's mouth as she could get as the orgasm rushed through every fiber of her body. Cardic bit her lip and rode the waves until she slid down the wall onto the small toilet seat. Cardic smiled weakly, trying to catch her breath, almost laughing at how stupid she must look.

Cardic opened her eyes and saw Iris righting her own clothes in the small mirror and checking her hair.

"Enjoy the rest of your flight, ma'am. Please return to your seat," Iris said as she leaned forward and placed a firm finger on Cardic's clitoris.

"Ah!" Cardic groaned and swatted her hand away. "Right

away." She grinned as Iris opened the small door and stepped out.

❖

Two months after her flight back home, school began. The start of a new semester always energized Cardic. Up early, she'd gotten a head start on planning the syllabus for her Intro to Cultural Studies class at Loyola. This was her third year teaching the class at Loyola, but unlike some of her colleagues, she changed her syllabus almost every year. The study of cultures was similar to a living, breathing thing. Always changing. Always surprising. The most important thing about being a professor for Cardic was sharing her passion for cultures with young people, seeing their minds change when understanding the lives of people so different from themselves.

Cardic was surprised at how easily she readjusted to her life and typical twenty-first-century comforts. Many colleagues told her they didn't feel at home for years after studying cultures in undeveloped areas of the world. The first few weeks proved the toughest. Her own bed seemed smothering and strange; the blankets would tangle and bunch, and most nights she found herself pushing them to the floor and sleeping with no cover at all, as she'd done in the jungle. The best thing about her return was access to a supply of cold, fresh water. Twice during her time with the Yanapo she had suffered from a waterborne illness. Since her return home, she'd taken to carrying a water bottle with her. She'd never take that for granted again.

Born and raised in Chicago, Cardic never thought much about the noise in the city, but that too had taken adjustment. Nighttime in the jungle had been her favorite, with the darkest sky and brightest stars imaginable, and the gentle rustle of leaves and branches along with the chirp of hundreds of nocturnal animals and insects she couldn't name. Never in her life had she felt so quiet and at peace.

She knew Chicago was home but felt changed from her time in the jungle. She had left Chicago eighteen months earlier as an anthropologist but returned as more of a whole person than she'd ever felt. She'd seen babies born, she'd learned another language, she'd hunted and killed her own food. A lifetime of experiences in a year and a half. Back in the States, she felt out of place, like a wild, country mouse who'd moved to the city. Getting back to work would help.

Cardic inhaled deeply as she glanced out of the bay window of her third-floor walk-up and rolled her shoulders. While out of the country, she had sublet her apartment to a young gay couple, and looking around the familiar neighborhood and surroundings made her glad she had. Her to-do list was getting longer by the day in preparation for the upcoming semester, and she couldn't imagine adding apartment hunting to that list.

The brick exterior and Juliet balconies on the upper floors gave the building character and charm. Other tenants had flower boxes, but Cardic didn't have the time or aptitude for plants. There was a rooftop deck that Cardic made use of during the summer months and covered parking in the back of the building, which could be hard to come by in many Chicago neighborhoods, especially Lincoln Park. Not that she needed it. Her apartment was less than four miles from the Water Tower Loyola campus, and it took her less than twenty minutes to get there on the Red Line train. There was a small dog park a few blocks away which made Cicero happy. Everything essential was within easy reach, and was also far enough away from Wrigley Field to make life during baseball season less hectic.

Cardic stopped in front of the boxes and boxes of notes

she had taken during her field study and ran her hands through her freshly cut hair. She shook her head, cringing at the thought of going through all the data. When she initially planned her field study, she knew analyzing and compiling eighteen months of data would be tedious, but she felt intimidated by the amount of work ahead of her. The data analysis, meetings with interdisciplinary colleagues, not to mention teaching four anthropology classes, was going to keep her calendar full.

Knowing her carefree days of summer were limited, Cardic put her coffee cup away and dressed for a run. After several days of humid and rainy weather, she knew a brisk run by the lakefront with its view of the skyline would be a productive way of releasing some pent-up energy. And Cardic never tired of watching beautiful women, and there should be plenty milling about today.

Cicero paced and bounced around as soon as he noticed Cardic lacing her running shoes. "Come on, boy, let's go." She rubbed his shaggy head as she grabbed her keys and sunglasses.

❖

"So, just stop by or email me with questions. If you need to extend a deadline, start looking for a new job." Olivia took a moment to thank the universe for sending her such capable and reliable employees as she glanced around at the staff of eager young professionals before her. She knew her statement about deadlines would be taken as it was. Not as a threat, but as fact. The release of the new athletic wear line was four months away, and she didn't have time for anyone who wasn't as focused and driven as she was. Olivia turned her attention to the whiteboard behind her and underlined the date of the release with a bright pink dry erase marker. "December twentieth. You can put your life on pause until this date."

After some basic questions, she dismissed her staff and sat at the head of the table. Standing during meetings was something she had always done, and she was positive any number of psychologists would give her some very deep reason as to why, but she wasn't all that interested. In a male-dominated field, she knew very well her presence had to be firm and commanding, and those weren't things she felt she could accomplish sitting down.

"Vivian, you stay."

"Yes, ma'am." Vivian, Olivia's executive assistant, sat back down and pulled out her tablet. She was young, hardworking, and completely obsessed with her job. Something Olivia liked and required in an employee. Vivian's Southern accent and sayings, while initially annoying, had surprisingly grown on Olivia. She was still trying to figure out how one was supposed to "mash" a button.

"Stop calling me ma'am. Did you schedule my flight to New York? And are we set to meet with the buyer from Bloomingdale's next Thursday?"

Vivian took a pencil from her hair and started taking notes on her ever-present yellow legal pad as she pulled up the calendar on her tablet. "Yes, ma'am. Olivia. Your flight leaves from O'Hare at seven thirty Monday morning. I found a flight Sunday evening, but I know you hate flying out of Midway. Harper and Ronald will meet with Bloomingdale's; the presentation is on your desk for review. Mr. Gentry from marketing called and wanted to confirm your lunch for today. And also you had two messages from Paul Nash regarding displays for the new line."

Paul was a longtime associate and product manager for an East Coast department store. Olivia knew he was interested in the new spring line of athletic wear from Vital, but she didn't plan on cutting any cost just because they were buddies. As the youngest brand manager in the history of the company, Olivia felt like too many people were waiting for her to make rookie mistakes like that. At thirty-one, she had no family, no pets, and no time or passion for anything but work. She knew she was going to succeed in making Vital the number three athletic wear company in the country within a few years, and not even a longtime friendship with someone like Paul was going to stand in her way.

"Excellent. Thanks, Vivian." In an uncharacteristic moment of praise and affection, Olivia patted Vivian on the shoulder as she walked out of the conference room. "You're doing great."

Vivian's efficiency and pleasant attitude were a welcome change from the last two assistants Olivia had let go. Vivian, a recent graduate of the University of Illinois, wanted to learn anything and everything she could. She kept up with Olivia's long hours, never called in sick, and remembered everything Olivia ever said. That kind of enthusiasm could be hard to find in someone in an entry-level position, so to secure Vivian as a part of the team she had negotiated her salary. Something Olivia rarely did.

After gathering her things, Vivian rushed out of the room to follow Olivia down the hall to her office. "You can call Mr. Gentry to confirm. I'll be going for a jog by the lake after we meet, so I won't be back until at least twelve thirty. I'll review Harper and Ronald's presentation then. Tell them I expect any changes ready by end of day." Vivian scribbled more notes on her legal pad and sat in one of the gray visitor's chairs flanking Olivia's desk. Olivia glanced around her sparse office as she pulled on her white blazer. The offices of Vital had been in this building in the East Loop of Chicago for nearly ten years. Most of the executives had deep mahogany furniture, classical art on the walls, and pictures of family on their desks.

Olivia's office was monotone gray, with minimal furniture, abstract art, and nothing on her desk but work. The rectangular space was small but suited its purpose. Olivia had room for a large file cabinet and two bookshelves. The large bank of floor-to-ceiling windows faced east, so on sunny days she had a flood of sunshine that was usually lost on her. Olivia stuffed her laptop in her charcoal shoulder bag and glanced at her desk, wondering if she should buy a plant or a knickknack.

When she was promoted to senior brand manager a year ago, she had brought very little from her even smaller office downstairs. Other than files, there wasn't much to bring. Olivia shook her head to clear the silly thought and tried to concentrate on the spew of information Vivian was hurling at her. A potted fern wasn't going to get her any closer to her goals. The space wasn't comfortable and didn't need to be. It was functional, uncluttered, and everything was within easy reach. In a brief moment of self-reflection, she remembered her bedroom during high school. Pictures of friends, a comfy beanbag chair, and books and magazines everywhere. When had her surroundings become so sterile?

"Oh, and the budget meeting was rescheduled for Wednesday, so I had to move your lunch with Joan to Friday."

"Fine, fine." Olivia grabbed her gym bag and headed toward the elevator, responding curtly to staff and coworkers who spoke to her as she went, Vivian close on her heels. "See you at twelve thirty. I'd like a copy of last year's gross profits on my desk when I return." Vivian was still scribbling notes as the elevator door closed, giving Olivia her first moment of peace since before six that morning.

The sushi bar that Sal Gentry had suggested was less than a mile away, and with the weather still mild, Olivia decided to walk rather than wait for the bus or hail a cab. Most meetings with the marketing team were held in the office, but Sal suggested they meet for lunch since he was swamped. Olivia reluctantly agreed. Even the minutes it took her to walk to the restaurant were a waste of valuable work time.

Olivia walked into the restaurant and was greeted by the hostess, who led her to one of the small square tables outside on the patio, where Sal was already seated. Annoyed that he'd taken the seat facing away from the sun, Olivia kept her large sunglasses in place and sat across from him.

"Olivia, thanks for meeting me. I'm sure you've got plenty of work to get done at the office, but I just needed some time away from the building. A change of scenery helps me think."

Olivia wondered at the easy way some people shared their thoughts and habits with others. By nature, Olivia was very private. She didn't even share her birthday with many people she worked with. "Of course, it's no trouble. Have you ordered?"

After some discussion, and Sal's enthusiastic suggestion, Olivia took Sal at his word and ordered the spicy tuna roll.

"So, I'll get right to it, Sal. We need some changes in marketing strategy. Up to this point, Vital has been the brand of white, middle-class golfers. Mr. McKinnon and the other stakeholders want to see something new. Something fresh. Something accessible. The launch of this new line is not only a new season but a relaunch of the Vital brand almost entirely. And with the addition of the plus-size line, we will be reaching a new demographic."

"Understood. My team has been working nearly nonstop. I don't think you or Mr. McKinnon will be disappointed with what we've come up with."

Olivia forced a smile. As the new brand manager of Vital, it was her job to create a line of athletic wear that everyone could relate to, that everyone wanted. The two largest athletic wear companies were institutions in America, and Olivia held no false hope of surpassing that success. She did have to remind herself that wasn't part of the job. Her job was to increase market share and brand loyalty. Olivia believed the key to this lay in the introduction of plus-size athletic wear from Vital. "Of course. I hope to see the full-page magazine ad by end of week."

"Absolutely. My apologies for the confusion about the sketches. We weren't under the impression that you wanted to feature plus-size models in the ad."

"Well, we couldn't exactly have someone who's a size two model a sports bra for someone who is a size eighteen, now could we?" Olivia's attempt at humor sounded much more like a sarcastic jab, but she couldn't bring herself to apologize or ease the wounded look on Sal's face.

"I meant no offense. I'm just an old-school marketing guy. We were taught the more Cindy Crawfords you could squeeze into an ad, the more product you'd sell." Sal's attempt at a joke only increased the awkwardness of the situation.

Olivia had been plus-size for most of her life and wasn't surprised or offended by the comment. "Well, body positivity and diversity in advertising are probably both here to stay, so let's roll with the punches. I want at least two plus-size girls in that ad."

After Sal inhaled his lunch, he headed back to the office, and Olivia breathed a sigh of relief. She'd always hated lunch meetings. Too much time wasted ordering and eating. After changing in the small bathroom of the restaurant, Olivia headed on foot down Diversey Parkway toward Lake Michigan. The heat was impressive, even for mid-August, and Olivia pulled a rubber band from the waistband pocket of her running pants. Olivia gathered her hair on top of her head, then secured the thick tangle and thought about how much curlier her hair was now in this humidity than it had been when she left her apartment that morning. After crossing the wide bike path of Lincoln Park, she stopped at a bench to stretch before taking off at an easy pace.

The sunshine felt warm but not oppressive as she traveled down the path of the harbor toward the lakefront. Olivia felt proud at the comfort and durability of the new Vital running shoes, and since she hadn't made it to the beach much this summer, she was glad to be wearing the lavender crop-top running shirt. There was still time to get a little sun on her midsection. As a size fourteen, she knew some people were surprised at the plus-size line of exercise and activewear from Vital, but women of all shapes and sizes deserved appropriate attire for all activities.

Olivia decided to try as hard as she could to push work from her mind as she broke out into a fast jog. She searched for her exercise playlist as she rounded one of the wide curves of the lakefront path.

Before she could register what happened, Olivia fell smack on her ass as a heavy, sweaty man hurled into her. At least this asshole had the courtesy to cradle her head during her fall so she wouldn't crack her skull on the concrete. Too pissed to speak, Olivia seethed as she took stock of her body and hoped nothing was seriously injured. Somewhere in the back of her mind, she realized this was no man but a very attractive woman with firm biceps—and reflexes like a cat. Olivia peeled her arms from the damp skin and pushed the thought from her mind and concentrated on her irritation.

"Can you get off?" Olivia squirmed under the oppressive weight of her assailant.

"I most certainly could." Cardic grinned down at the face that was almost as breathtaking as the full breasts that were squashed against her sweaty T-shirt. "Cardic," she offered as she lifted her chest and locked her elbows, making no move to get up.

"Suffocating," responded the redheaded beauty, unmoving but annoyed beneath her. Cardic was lost in the bright green pools of her eyes, accented by the red of her hair and the pink of her cheeks. Her narrow brows furrowed together as Cicero approached and licked her face. It struck Cardic as unfair that Cicero would get the first crack at her.

"Cicero, back," Cardic said as she got to her feet and offered her hand to the woman. Cardic suppressed a smile as the annoyed woman stood and pulled an earbud from her sports bra. Cardic loved breasts as much as the next lesbian, but damn if this wasn't the best pair she'd ever laid eyes on. The woman had a solid D cup at least, with a slim waist and rounded hips. Cardic was tempted to stroll around the woman just to get a look at her from all angles. Surely her ass was just as impressive. Her skin was a little darker than Cardic would have expected for a redhead, but not by much. Skin glistening with just a hint of perspiration, smooth, and unblemished. This woman's entire body was just…sex. Sex dressed in black and lavender spandex.

"I'm sorry. I didn't get your name," Cardic said as the woman pierced her with a vicious glare.

"No, you got me dirty," she snapped as she brushed away the invisible dirt she must have been referring to.

"Dirty isn't necessarily a bad thing," Cardic joked as she threw Cicero's tennis ball a few feet away.

Olivia's eyes tracked the shaggy, kissing dog as he trotted off after his ball. "You don't keep him on a leash?"

"No need. He goes where I go," Cardic replied. Now in a vertical position, Olivia felt a little less off-kilter as she took stock of the woman. She was androgynous with a tall, lanky build and small breasts. Olivia could see why she had mistaken her for a man at first. She had a jaw like an anvil, and if Cardic were more feminine, Olivia might have assumed she'd had collagen injected into those beautiful lips. Somehow she didn't seem the type.

"He goes where you go? I can't imagine why." Olivia rolled her eyes, almost surprised at her own rudeness.

"Look, I'm sorry I ran you over. Can I make it up to you? Dinner tonight?"

Olivia nearly laughed. The idea was absurd. Letting her eyes roam over Cardic's body, the subtly bulging biceps, the easy, casual posture, she had to remind herself *why* it was absurd. *Oh, work.* Yes, of course. She'd be at the office until at least nine tonight. Not to mention the fact that she wasn't about to let some hot butch woman try to top her in the bedroom. Olivia tried to ignore the hitch in her breath as she pushed the image from her mind. "No, I don't think so."

"What? Why not?" Cardic seemed confused, her brows knitting together. Apparently, she wasn't used to being turned down. Then a lazy grin spread across her handsome face. "Straight?"

"Aside from the fact that you practically just gave me a concussion, I have plans. And based on our first encounter, I'm not sure I could survive an evening in your accident-prone company." Her annoyance at this stranger was growing. Olivia glanced at her watch and cursed, realizing she wouldn't make it back to the office until at least one o'clock due to this little accident.

"Can I at least get your name?" Cardic followed a few steps as Olivia jogged away.

"Olivia."

CHAPTER TWO

*O*livia.

Cardic closed her eyes, pushed Olivia from her mind, and again tried to convince herself it was pointless to lament over her. With almost three million people in Chicago, she knew the odds of ever running into the feisty redhead again were slim to none. Especially after jogging the same trail the following three days and not seeing her again. Not that she'd admit that to anyone.

"Dr. Lawson, do you want these profiles separated by birth date or gender? What are you going for here?" Patrick, Cardic's graduate assistant and friend, poked his head in from the outer office and held up several of the profile cards Cardic had completed on all the tribe members of the Yanapo. She'd enlisted his help to get all her data organized before she dove in. To move through analyzing the data in the most efficient way possible, she needed to know exactly where everything would be and in what order.

"First gender, then sub-sort by birth date."

"You got it, Doc." Patrick scurried back to his purple zebra-print office chair. Cardic detested the thing, but Patrick insisted the office needed some flair.

The beginning of the fall semester was fast approaching,

and Cardic found herself torn between her usual excitement about a new school year and wanting to be completely absorbed in the mountains of data she needed to get through for her ethnography.

Her interest in the Yanapo tribe had begun in 2007 when she read an article by one of her favorite cultural anthropologists, Fredrick Simpson. During his fourth field study of the Yanomami tribe, he noticed a slight difference in the dialect of the tribe the farther southeast he traveled within the tribe's territory. While the same could be said for dialects in many areas, Simpson felt the shift was so strong it almost became a different language altogether. Determined to figure it out, Simpson led a massive uncharted hike deep into the Rio Pure National Park. Lo and behold, within three months, the man had discovered an uncontacted native tribe—the Yanapo. This late in the game, it was nearly unheard of for uncontacted tribes to still be in existence.

This alone wasn't the most interesting part of the discovery for Cardic. Simpson also reported that the Yanapo were a completely non-monogamous civilization with no marriage ceremony of any kind, unlike most neighboring tribes. Unlike most societies and cultures in general. How was it that a tribe like this had been able to remain cloistered away in the recesses of the jungle and defy some of the most basic norms of established civilizations? Cardic had to know.

After finishing her dissertation and securing a position as a professor of cultural anthropology at Loyola, Cardic made the necessary plans for her own field study. Now, three years later, having completed eighteen months of in-depth field study, Cardic was eager to analyze her data and begin writing her ethnography. Two other anthropologists had completed field studies with the Yanapo after the discovery of their existence and published ethnographies on the tribe. These ethnographies, like most, gave a general overview of the culture: day-to-day activities, customs, and ritual practices. Unlike them, Cardic's ethnography would dive deep into the rarest aspects of the tribe—the lack of a marriage ceremony or monogamous relationships between adult members of the tribe.

"Did you choose a textbook for 101 yet? Department head says he needs the info by Monday," Patrick said from the doorway as he sipped a coffee. Apparently, he was taking another break.

"Which one was the cheapest on that list I gave you?" Cardic hated choosing a textbook. None of her syllabus material came from a book anyway. But alas, rules were rules.

"*Intro to Anthro*, the same one as last semester." Patrick squinted and pursed his lips as if trying to remember correctly.

"Fine, then," Cardic grumbled, moving toward the outer office bookshelf to flip through the book in question.

"Don't be such a rebel. The course has to have a text." Patrick slapped her playfully on the stomach as she passed. "Damn, honey! You been doing crunches?" He shook his hand as if it hurt.

"You'd be surprised how much hunting with a bow and arrow works your core." Cardic ran her fingers along the bookshelf, skimming the titles, and realized she had learned more during her time with the Yanapo than she had ever learned from any book.

"Well, you look great, doll. Any other body modifications I should know about?" Patrick headed back to the box of cards and continued to sort.

Cardic rubbed the spot on her chest just above her right breast and felt a moment of protectiveness over her newly healed tattoo. During her research of the Yanapo, she learned of their tattoo ceremonies in which young men and women were declared of age. On the night before she left the tribe, they held a surprise ceremony in her honor. The tattoo process was lengthy and painful. Cardic recalled gritting her teeth and balling her fists as Taya, one of the tribesmen, had hammered the design into her flesh with a sharp stick. Lying next to the fire on a woven grass mat, sweat had dampened her skin. Cardic tried to figure out how she was ever going to convey the experience in words.

"Just the usual."

The phone ringing ripped Cardic from her musings, and she continued to hunt for the textbook.

"Dr. Lawson's office," Patrick answered in a cheery voice. "One moment." Patrick covered the receiver and mouthed, "She sounds cute."

Cardic rolled her eyes and grabbed the phone. "Lawson."

"Hi, Cardic. It's Meredith. Glad I caught you."

Cardic's stomach turned. She and Meredith had met several weeks ago at a Greek festival in Andersonville. They'd spent an enjoyable evening in bed, and Cardic had explained beforehand that was all it would be. Before jumping into bed, they had made small talk, and Cardic must have let her occupation slip. That was the only way Meredith could have tracked her down.

"Meredith. How are you?" Cardic always tried to treat her lovers with respect and honesty. And she rarely ran into trouble. Women who played by her rules were rewarded with what she considered her sexual expertise. But some women wanted to tame her, in spite of her honest warnings and objections. She guessed Meredith was in this category.

"Well, I'm doing fine. Just wondering when we can get together again." Cardic could tell Meredith was trying her hardest to be sexy, but it sounded forced.

"Thanks for the offer, but it's just not a good time now."

Cardic breathed deeply through her nose, trying her hardest not to be annoyed.

"So you…I mean…so that's it, then?"

"It's not you." Cardic faced the window and lowered her voice. "I had a blast, but like I said before, I'm not really interested in anything more." Patrick knew the sordid details of Cardic's love life, but she wanted to somehow protect Meredith's dignity.

"Did you let this one down gently?" Patrick whined as Cardic stalked back into her office.

"I'm sure she'll be fine," Cardic grumbled as she powered up her laptop and closed the two large windows in her office. After turning on the small fan in the corner, she walked back to her desk. It was still too warm to be without air-conditioning, and Cardic's skin was itching for fall.

"Well, who's next on the hit list?" Patrick wasn't exactly celibate, so Cardic wondered about the sudden interest in her love life. At the same time, her mind flashed to Olivia, the wild redheaded beauty.

"Ran into a girl, quite literally, when I was out with Cicero, but she blew me off."

"Straight?"

"Not a chance." Something about the confident way Olivia carried herself, her poise and demeanor, and the not-so-shy appraisal of Cardic's body told her she was at least bisexual. Cardic thought again and realized there was no way a woman like Olivia would bend for any man, or any woman, for that matter.

"Well, what went wrong? Not many women can resist your charms."

"I don't know, but I can't get her out of my head." Cardic rubbed her temples, irritated at her inability to forget the feisty creature. And she had no idea how to find her.

❖

Olivia uncapped her water bottle and took a large gulp as she flexed her hand. Carpal tunnel or any variation of the disorder was not in her career plan. After grabbing the stress ball that rested neatly next to her keyboard, she clicked back through the deck she needed ready by next week. The brain-shaped stress ball had been a graduation gift from her father. Olivia dug her nails into the small grooves and realized it had been more meaningful and useful than any of the fancy pens or letter openers she had received.

She'd been active in sports throughout her childhood and played on the varsity softball team for two years, but her father always maintained that her sharp wit and unstoppable intellect would be what propelled her to success.

The pressure to succeed was something Olivia supposed she'd been born with. Her father never pushed her or had anything to say other than the most encouraging of words. Even before her mother left when Olivia was six, she had still felt the need to surpass all the kids around her in every area, going so far as to fight with the boys.

The last time she got in a fight, she'd been nine and Daniel Rodriguez had pushed her down the top step of the apartment she and her father lived in. She recalled lying on the sidewalk, trying desperately to catch her breath after having the wind knocked out of her, rage cooking inside her body.

Not unlike just recently being knocked down during her jog by that tall drink of water. *Cardic.* She had to admit that the sensation running through her body after that encounter was less like rage and more like curiosity.

At that thought, Olivia set the stress ball back in its

rightful place and let her eyes drift shut. As she leaned back in her leather chair, she pictured Cardic. Smiling a cocky smile.

Olivia couldn't recall the last time a woman had caught her attention. Two months ago at least. Francesca? Or was it Frances? Not that it mattered. Occasional company with a willing woman was enough to satisfy her basic sexual needs. The romance, the puppy-dog eyes, the drama, and the emotions were things she could do without. Not that Cardic seemed the romantic type in the least.

Olivia assumed Cardic had a harem that could fill Wrigley Field. The image of Cardic in a candlelit setting with that tousled hair and lazy smile flashed through Olivia's mind. Those cocoa-colored eyes could probably strip most women's clothes off.

"Not mine." Olivia snorted as she swirled her chair around to reach the mini fridge. Alcohol wasn't something she typically kept in the office, but she pulled out a grape-flavored vodka and a small shot glass from her desk drawer and enjoyed the burn and numbing effect of a shot before heading home.

Olivia hailed a cab rather than making the six-block walk to the Red Line train in her wool blazer. *Too early for wool.*

"Going somewhere special?" the cabbie asked as she dumped her bag in the seat next to her.

"No, just home." Olivia rubbed her temples as she gave her address and instructed the driver to avoid LaSalle Street because of the construction she'd seen on the bus that morning.

Somewhere special. Where might that be? It didn't matter. What mattered was work, and that was going perfectly. A ripple of concern and nervousness ran through Olivia's body. Why the sudden unrest? Everything was going right. She had an amazing staff that worked their asses off, the spring line for Vital was sure to be a hit, and she was in perfect health.

Maybe it *had* been too long since she'd been with a woman. That would be the only logical explanation for her unease. When things died down at work, Olivia decided she would seek out some female company—but not until then. Usually, running on less than four hours' sleep didn't leave energy for much else. Especially something she enjoyed putting energy into such as sex.

Decidedly feminine, Olivia often found herself on the receiving end of attention from men. It wasn't surprising. But early on in life, she found herself attracted to very feminine women. She had every respect for those who identified as bisexual, but when seeking out bedroom partners, for her, the closer to straight they were, the better. They were always eager for sex and experience but very wary of anything outside the bedroom. Which suited Olivia perfectly. Have a good time, and let them scurry off to their boyfriends. It was easier to control her encounters that way.

Being in control of everything around her was exhausting, but taking control in the bedroom was easy.

Yet another reason to remove the lingering thoughts of Cardic from her mind. Olivia would bet her corner office that Cardic was always in control when it came to sex.

Chapter Three

L oyola requires that I assign a textbook for this course. You won't need it. This is a discussion-based course. Which brings me to attendance. Loyola also has an attendance policy. I don't. You're paying to be here. If you don't want to come, it's no business of mine, but passing will be difficult if you don't take part in our discussions." Cardic stood at the front of the small classroom addressing her new students. One young man in the back timidly raised his hand.

"So, should we buy the textbook or not?"

"Up to you." Cardic walked back to her desk and picked up her notepad to glance at the book info. "It's your money. But I can think of a few things I'd rather spend that on. Especially after a two-hour Thursday evening class."

That got a chuckle from her students. Not foolish enough to think things had changed much since her undergraduate days at a small liberal arts college, Cardic had a pretty good idea what these kids did over the weekend. Cardic finished up going over the syllabus and dismissed her new class.

As she packed up for the day, she glanced at the clock. Claire would be waiting for her across the street for lunch, and she still had to swing by her office to get her laptop. After closing the classroom door, she was surprised to see Patrick sprinting toward her.

"Hey, Doc, you left your laptop upstairs," Patrick said, out of breath. The look on his face said something was up.

"I was on my way up. I'm going to meet Claire. What's that look for?" Cardic raised an eyebrow, and she tucked the small computer in her brown leather shoulder bag, pulling out her ever-present water bottle to make room.

"Davenport's on the warpath. He already laid into Melanie about not using his textbook in her sociology class. Pretty sure he'll chew you out if he finds out you recommended, again, that the kids don't buy textbooks."

Cardic chucked. Cory Davenport was the assistant department head, a position she was pretty sure he made up for himself, being a micromanager and a pain in her ass. "Well, good thing I just suggested they spend that money on alcohol instead."

Patrick's dark skin paled. "You didn't?"

"Not in so many words. Don't look so worried, Pat. I can talk my way out of anything." Cardic grinned as she locked the classroom door behind her.

"Yeah, except being late to meet Claire. If I see Davenport, I'll just claim I don't know you. Kiss that baby for me."

She gave Patrick a gentle shoulder bump, then jogged down the hall to the elevator. Cardic loved working at the Chicago Loyola campus. First, she was close to home and didn't need to drive to work, and she loved being in a city that always had something to keep her occupied. Second, her sister and nephew could meet her for lunch or come over for dinner a couple of times a week.

Cardic unbuttoned the cuffs of her sleeves and rolled them up to her elbows. Her skin was still a golden brown from all the months she'd spent in the sun with the Yanapo. There were subtle reminders of her time there all around her. Her brown skin, the desire to sprint everywhere she needed to go, her inability to even look at junk food.

Walking toward Daisy's Kitchen, the café on the corner of Pearson and Rush where she and Claire met once a week, Cardic glanced in the mirrored windows at herself as she walked. Other than the tan and her healed chest tattoo, nothing about her outward appearance suggested she had gone through a life-changing experience.

At times, she felt unprofessional because of the way she was emotionally affected by and connected to this group of people. As a scientist, it was important for her to be objective and observe the culture. But after being a part of their celebrations, witnessing births, helping to bury their dead, she felt a kindred connection to the people and their culture.

And all data was good data. The sooner she could dive into it, the better.

Cardic was shocked by the cool rush of air as she stepped into the restaurant and removed her sunglasses. Air-conditioning continued to be a source of awe since her return to the States, just like running water.

"Cardic, over here," Claire called in a happy voice from their favorite table in the corner. Daisy's Kitchen was a quiet diner with kind of a fifties nostalgia about it. There were framed Elvis records on the walls and a Marilyn Monroe statue next to the long soda bar. If it weren't for the amazing chicken salad sandwich, Cardic would have detested the place based on the décor alone.

Cardic grabbed a menu from the bar as she came over, and Clark, her three-year-old nephew, whined to get down from his high chair and greet her.

"Auntie, I got a hot dog!" The boy toddled toward her, and she picked him up, pretending to take a bite from his half-eaten dog. "No, Auntie, mine!" He laughed as she placed him back in his seat.

"How was class? Dreamy-eyed girls hogging the front row?" Claire hugged Cardic and ruffled her hair.

Cardic rolled her eyes. She'd never noticed any fawning from her female students. By definition, anthropologists weren't typically head turners. They were usually nerdy bookworm types who wore khakis and sweater vests and read *National Geographic*. While Cardic might not fit into the typical look of an anthropologist, she could certainly sport a sweater vest in the fall and had a vintage collection of *National Geographics* on her bookshelf.

The female student body had never shown any overt interest in her. Thank God. Cardic loved women but didn't want any awkward encounters with students who were much too young and much too off-limits.

"But really, hon, you've been home for what, a couple of months? We've seen you every weekend. No lady love at the moment?" Claire dipped a napkin into her water and gently dabbed at Clark's ketchup-smeared cheeks.

"What's the rush? There's plenty of women and plenty of time." As soon as the words left her mouth, Cardic felt sick. "Shit, Claire, I'm sorry. That was stupid."

"Watch your mouth. And just stop. I'm fine. Clark and I are better off. It's getting easier. Please don't censor yourself because you fear for my feelings." Claire looked at her with an expression of tenderness.

"How is the sperm donor?" Cardic gritted her teeth and looked away from her. It hurt just to know that she was hurting from anything. When Claire had broken her wrist roller-skating in fourth grade, Cardic was only seven, but she couldn't even look at Claire's cast. They were as close as siblings could get, and Cardic felt an empathetic connection to her older sister. When Claire hurt, she hurt. Physically or otherwise.

"He wants more visitation. I don't know why. Clark doesn't even want to see him. Plus, we just worked out a schedule that works perfectly. I think he just likes to mess with me."

"What does your lawyer advise?"

"We're waiting until the next court date to renegotiate the schedule."

Turning to Clark, Cardic put on her happiest face and said loudly, "Well, someone is turning four soon."

"It's me, Auntie. I'm three, but I want to be four."

"And you will, darling. A little over a month. Who do you want to come to your birthday party?" Claire asked as she continued to eat her own lunch now that Clark had finished and was playing with his toys.

"You, Mommy. And Auntie. And my friends. But not Daddy, okay?"

Claire's eyes watered. "No, you'll have another party with Daddy and Samantha." Clark looked at Claire and made a mad face.

"Wow, you get two birthday parties? What a cool guy you are," Cardic jumped in, wanting to avoid any talk of her cheating ex-brother-in-law or his new girlfriend, knowing that Claire was wearing a brave face, but even speaking the other woman's name must be torture. At the mention of two parties, Clark perked up a little and continued to play with his cars.

"Please tell me some happy news. Make it up if you have to." Claire laughed awkwardly as the waitress came over to take Cardic's order.

"Chicken salad sandwich," Cardic said without looking up, handing the woman her menu.

"Pickles?" the woman asked.

Cardic looked up, realizing no one at Daisy's had ever asked if she wanted pickles with her sandwich. The playful smile on the waitress's face made her wonder if that was just an excuse to get her attention.

"Would you recommend the pickles?" Cardic's mouth quirked and she casually laid her arm on the back of the chair next to her, stretching out her frame.

As the waitress's eyes moved down her body, she could feel her dry spell coming to an end. Maybe it was time for some fun.

The younger woman nodded.

"I'll trust your opinion, then." Cardic winked as the woman returned her smile and walked away with an impressive sway of her hips.

"You're an animal. She's too young. What if she goes to Loyola?"

Cardic laughed, knowing the girl was too young but still enjoying the flirting. "Relax. I'm not interested."

"That's a relief. But seriously, you're not dating anyone right now? No one you want to bring to the party?"

While Cardic and her sister were close, Claire didn't really understand or know the extent of Cardic's liaisons. Cardic didn't date. And she never would. If she was spending time with a woman, it was for sex and sex alone. There had been a few times she'd brought a woman home to meet her family, but it was more to please her mother or quiet Claire's curiosity.

"Nope. No one at the moment. No interests." At that, an image of Olivia crossed her mind. *Damn it.* When was the redheaded siren going to vacate her subconscious?

"Well, I guess since she can't get through to you, Mom has started trying to convince *me* that you need to settle down."

Cardic would do anything for her mother or her family, other than getting married. She had seen the social construct of monogamy nearly ruin the lives of the two most important women in her life. She'd be damned if she was going to let it ruin her own. It was hopeless to try to convince them eternal love didn't exist, but she didn't have to spend her life searching for the elusive emotion.

As a scientific observer, trying to stay objective when it came to her own family was difficult. But she knew her sister's and mother's fairy-tale notions and naïve belief that "love can conquer all" were the reasons they had both suffered so much at the hands of the men in their lives. These were beliefs she kept to herself. No need to add insult to injury.

After the conversation moved on to more pleasant topics, and Clark fell asleep against Claire's arm, the waitress came over to clear their plates and left the bill facedown.

"So we'll see you Saturday for Clark's game?" Claire hefted the heavy toddler onto her hip and grabbed her purse.

Clark had just started playing soccer. Cardic didn't even know three-year-olds knew how to play soccer. And based on his last game, they didn't. It was more like a bunch of adults on the sidelines yelling at kids to get the ball while taking pictures of the chaos.

"Count me in." Cardic smiled, and her heart warmed; she'd take any excuse to spend time with Clark.

Claire picked up the bill and laughed. "I guess lunch is on you today."

Cardic grabbed the bill and glanced at the feminine handwriting with a phone number written under the total. Cardic shook her head and kissed her sister, tossed some bills on the table, and headed out of Daisy's, avoiding the young waitress.

Chapter Four

So do you want me to pick you up? Are you going to take the L?" Joan, Olivia's best friend and polar opposite, sat across from her at the swanky bar as they shared a late dinner.

"I'll probably just head over straight from work." Olivia picked up a mushroom and kale pot sticker and took a bite.

"Just make sure you're dressed to kill, okay?" Joan's wrist jingled with bracelets as she signaled to the bartender that she needed another Moscow mule.

"Me, dressed to kill? You're the one spinning for the event; why does it matter what I wear?"

"Because you'll be with me, and I want us both to look amazing. Maybe you can attract some hot men for me since I'll be behind the record table."

Olivia knew Joan was excited, even though she was always excited. Something about this event was making her mania a little more intense than usual. Olivia sipped her martini and nodded for Joan to continue.

"So the boat leaves at seven thirty, but I'm supposed to be on board by seven. Sorry, you'll have to wait in line. I asked about some sort of VIP pass, but Gary, the event organizer, he said since tickets are so hard to come by, the whole deal is kind of VIP."

"I don't mind, especially since it's for charity. I'll just see you when I get on board."

Spinning on the "booze cruise" was a big break for Joan, and Olivia couldn't have been more proud of her. She'd been an up-and-coming DJ at electronic dance clubs around Chicagoland for several years, but this was the first time she'd been asked to do an event this large outside the EDM scene. Spinning didn't pay the bills, but Joan loved it and had to suffer through her daytime job as a paralegal.

Olivia had met Joan at St. Augustus when she was a sophomore. As outcasts, they had clicked instantly. Olivia the poor, chubby redhead and Joan, the tall, bleach-blond punk. Joan had been kicked out of St. Augustus junior year for smoking in the bathroom, but they'd stayed friends.

Olivia had changed a lot since high school, but something about Joan had stayed carefree and youthful. Her hair was similar to the spikes she'd worn when younger, only now the short waves had a softer, feminine look. Olivia realized Joan still had an entirely black wardrobe as she glanced at her black scoop-neck tee.

"Are you nervous?" Olivia placed her napkin on the table.

"Hell no. Well, yes. Let's talk about something else. How's work?" Joan spat out in one breath.

"Work's great. Busy of course. The other day I got an email from—"

"Yeah, that's awesome. What about the lady scene? Any developments there?" Joan sipped her mule and acted casual as she attempted to change the subject.

Olivia knew her job could come across as boring to someone who wasn't into marketing or retail, so she excused Joan's dismissal. But she wasn't in the mood for the conversation that usually followed.

"No, no developments. Other than the eye candy I bumped

into while running, I haven't even seen a woman worth looking at—"

"Back up. What eye candy? When was this?" Joan squealed.

Shit. It occurred to Olivia that she had intentionally not mentioned this to Joan. Why she had let it slip now, she had no idea.

"Ah, it was nothing. I was just out for a jog a couple of weeks ago and bumped into this hot butch chick."

"Butch? That's new for you. Please, continue." Joan lifted an eyebrow and studied Olivia's face.

Olivia replayed the events, leaving out the unwelcome arousal that had followed her around for days afterward.

"Are you going to see her again?"

"No, no way. It was just a chance meeting. We didn't exchange numbers. I doubt I'll see her again."

"Dammit, Olivia." Joan smacked her hand on the smooth surface of the high table.

Olivia looked at her with shock. "What? I don't go jogging to pick up chicks, you know."

"Well, maybe you should. You need to cut loose, Olive. I don't know if you need a break from work, or sex, or a bong hit, but you need to cut this shit out."

"What shit are you talking about?" Olivia was confused. Things were going great. Things were taking off at work. Her dad was in good health. She and Joan saw each other at least once a week. "What?"

"Fun. You need some. I know you love work, and in your warped, control-freak brain, that's somehow fun, but I'm talking about real fun. Where you just enjoy yourself and don't worry about the end product or the outcome. I bet you came here straight from the office, too, didn't you?" Joan eyed the black briefcase resting at Olivia's feet.

Slightly embarrassed, Olivia avoided Joan's eyes. "Guilty as charged. Where's this coming from, Joan?"

For a moment, Joan grew still. She met Olivia's eyes as she reached into her clutch bag and pulled out a crumpled newspaper clipping. "Do you remember Adam Stills?" Adam was a boy they both knew in high school. He attended the male counterpart to their all-girls Catholic school. Before Olivia even realized she was a lesbian, she and Joan would always try to pick up guys from St. Bart's.

"Yes, of course. He beat my SAT score. I haven't spoken to him in a few years. Why?" Joan handed over the clipping. It was an obituary from July.

"Heart attack. He was only thirty-three. Like you, he had some kind of high-stress, high-stakes corporate gig. No kids, no pets, nothing but his job and a wife he probably never saw. Is this going to be you?" Joan looked on the verge of tears.

"Joan, I'm perfectly healthy." Olivia tried to brush off the concern and the eerie similarities to her own life and the life she read in the obituary.

"You're missing the point. If you died tomorrow because of a career you loved, then so be it. But did you enjoy anything? There's so much more to life, Olive. Please promise me you'll try. Try to have some fun. Please."

Olivia was in shock. Joan by nature played things close to the chest just like Olivia herself. Where was this coming from? And why did Olivia feel like she was back in high school with her head in a book on prom night? Was she really forgoing some kind of transient pleasure because she worked seventy-hour weeks?

"Olive! Promise." Joan interrupted her thoughts with a pinch to her wrist.

"Yes. I promise."

❖

Olivia took a calming breath as she rushed down the sidewalk toward the L station. Last night, at Joan's insistence, Olivia had tried to "let loose." Instead of ironing her work shirt the night before like she had done since her first job right out of college, she let it hang in the closet as she drank another glass of wine and flipped through reality TV. The anxiety was mild enough that she was able to sleep but completely threw off her morning routine.

Olivia cursed as she pulled up the transit app on her phone, realizing she'd have to take the next train. There was no way she could make the half-mile walk to the station in heels in less than three minutes.

Olivia slowed to a brisk walk and tried to remember why she agreed to entertain the silly notion of more fun in her life. *Oh yeah, because of Joan's dramatic and alarmist plea for my health.*

Olivia mentally cataloged the list of healthy things in her life. When she thought of jogging, she stopped. She recalled her last jog by the lake. And Cardic. A tingle ran down her spine and settled in her belly as she thought of Cardic's hard body and knowing smile. Olivia realized she had only been jogging in her neighborhood or near work every day since then to avoid running into her again.

And what if she had said yes to Cardic's invitation to dinner? Would they have gone out on a real date or headed straight for dessert? Her now-active imagination conjured up something to do with cherries and licking a trail of chocolate syrup off Cardic's chest and stomach.

Whoa. Where did that come from?

Crossing the street and heading for the stairs of the train station, Olivia tried to remove Cardic completely from her mind.

She hoped tomorrow's booze cruise would distract her from her decadent thoughts and maybe even bring about some more appropriate possible bed partners. Olivia realized her libido had been in overdrive since meeting Cardic. Though she'd promised herself no sex until after the launch of the new Vital line, maybe just one night of blissful release to take the edge off wouldn't hurt.

Chapter Five

Olivia grabbed the railing underneath the window and tried to stop her head from spinning. Seasick? Olivia Reynolds did not get seasick. *Must be something I ate.* In the small hallway, away from the loud music and dancing bodies, the sway of the boat was much more noticeable. Olivia concentrated on the clink of her scarlet fingernails against the brass railing as she waited for her turn in the bathroom.

Joan's set had been amazing. The crowd cheered and jumped up to dance with almost every song she played. Most of the songs were recent top forty hits, but Joan even threw in some early nineties stuff. She knew how to keep the crowd excited, and so far, more people were up dancing than sitting at any of the dining tables around the perimeter of the dance floor.

The cruise was a charity event to raise money for a local Chicago organization against gun violence. Olivia was always happy to donate to charity. Peering around the throng of people waiting for the bathroom, she caught sight of Joan. Olivia winked at her as their eyes met. Joan gave her a goofy thumbs-up and went back to her computer to change the song.

As the boat took a sudden sway to the left, Olivia was almost knocked off balance. She grabbed the railing to right herself and murmured a thank-you to the person passing who grabbed her elbow.

The hand kept holding and then squeezing gently, and Olivia peered up into the brownest eyes she'd ever seen. When she'd been pinned underneath Cardic at the lake, she noticed small flecks of gold in her deep brown eyes. But now, in the dim light of the hallway, her eyes looked the color of rich, dark roast coffee beans. "Falling for me again?" Cardic's voice was slow and sexy, and only loud enough for her to hear.

"You wish," Olivia snapped, trying to appear unaffected by those eyes and the strong but gentle grip on her arm. She fleetingly thanked the universe she'd worn a cardigan so she couldn't feel Cardic's warm skin pressed against hers.

Cardic couldn't believe her luck. When Patrick suggested she join him on the booze cruise, she'd been hesitant. Her mile-long to-do list wasn't getting any shorter, and she had her 101 class's first papers to grade this weekend. But the nagging feeling that she should be somewhere else completely disappeared the moment she spotted Olivia from across the room.

Lady Luck was on her side again when the boat swayed as she approached, and she was again able to catch this siren in her arms. Sort of. Cardic would have been more pleased if somehow Olivia had fallen and they'd both ended up naked in her bed. But the night was young. "Have dinner with me," Cardic said.

"I already ate."

"Not tonight. Come on. You know you want to." Cardic boldly let her finger trail up the woman's arm toward her shoulder. "I can see it in those very green eyes of yours."

"I've actually gotta go. Early morning tomorrow." She

backed away from Cardic and scooted toward the dance floor, where she backed into the DJ.

"You are not leaving yet. My set's only halfway over—" The DJ's eyes landed on Cardic. "Hell-o. I'm Joan, Olivia's best friend. Friend only. Just friend." Joan winked at Olivia as she extended her hand to an amused Cardic.

"I've enjoyed your set so far. I'm Cardic."

"Oh, lakefront, accident-prone eye candy. Excellent."

Cardic's eyebrows shot up in pleased surprise as she shook Joan's hand. "Guilty as charged."

"Look, Joan, I'm sure you don't want to stand around and talk on your break. Let's go check out the view before you have to go back on."

"Actually, I wanna dance. Come on, Cardic," Joan said happily, pulling Cardic by the hand.

Grin still in place, Cardic followed Joan to the dance floor, not looking back at Olivia.

On the dance floor, Cardic was impressed with Joan's moves, but why should she be? Music was part of her career, after all.

She could no longer see Olivia when she glanced back at the hallway and thought it might be safe to ask the question she'd been begging to ask since Joan dragged her away.

As she spun Joan around and looked down into her eyes, Cardic just threw it out there. "Anything you can do to help me out here?"

"You don't seem the type to ask for help," Joan joked, wrapping her arm around Cardic's waist as the music bumped a little faster.

"Not usually the kind that needs it." Cardic pulled Joan a little closer, hoping Olivia was watching. She'd do just about anything at this point to get her attention.

The song ended, and a leggy blond sidled up to Cardic requesting the next dance. Joan backed up out of the way and laughed, heading back to the booth. "I'll put in a good word for you," she called. "You'll need it."

Cardic eyed the blonde and regarded her carefully. She was tall and a little too thin for Cardic's taste, and after just a look at Olivia, her nerves were on fire. A hot dance with a willing woman was probably not a smart idea.

"What's your name, baby?" the blonde asked, close to her ear.

"Cardic."

"I'm Jen. A friend of Patrick's." The woman winked and tilted her head toward the restroom. "He said your girl could use some inspiration."

Cardic caught sight of Olivia heading back toward her table with an unamused expression on her face. Her body was lithe and supple, and she wore a skintight black dress with a deep purple cardigan covering her shoulders and arms. The dark tones highlighted the natural glow of her skin, and Cardic ached to expose every inch of that creamy flesh.

Just as Jen pumped her ass into Cardic's crotch with the music, Olivia's eyes locked on Cardic's. Cardic's hips gyrated in time with the music, and it had nothing to do with the woman she was dancing with. Her eyes never left Olivia's as she ran her hand up and down Jen's side, grazing the underside of her breast, praying the woman in her arms would transform into Olivia.

Olivia's expression had been hard to read a moment ago, but now as her eyes tracked the movement of Cardic's hands, she seemed almost angry. At least Cardic had her attention.

Score one for Team Cardic.

Cardic closed her eyes and dipped her head to rub her face

in Jen's fragrant hair, wondering what Olivia's hair smelled like. Shampoo. Hair spray. Sweat.

When Cardic opened her eyes, Olivia was headed straight for them. Jen swiveled around and whispered, "Is that her? She looks pissed. I'm out." She pressed her lips none too subtly against Cardic's before walking through the crowd.

Though Olivia's body called to her like a magnet, Cardic made a show of watching Jen leave. Cocky grin in place, she turned her attention to Olivia. Olivia's arms were crossed under her ample breasts, her hip jutted out, and her patent leather heel was tapping the dance floor.

"Can I speak with you?"

"Of course." Cardic waved her arm for Olivia to precede her to the outer deck.

"Look, I don't know what, if anything, Joan said to you, but I don't—"

"Not much. Just that I'd need help if I wanted your attention. But it looked like I had it a moment ago."

Olivia scoffed. *Self-righteous little...* She couldn't help the burn in her gut at the sight of Cardic with her arms around that Carmen Diaz doppelgänger. Olivia pushed the strange sensation aside and concentrated on her annoyance at Cardic's continued and unwanted presence in her life.

"Listen, I've already said I don't want dinner, okay? Now please just...go away."

As a noisy group of twentysomethings pushed by toward the staircase, Cardic leaned in close to Olivia's ear. "It doesn't have to be dinner."

Olivia grabbed on to her anger and annoyance to avoid the tightness that settled in her belly with this sensual creature so close to her. Cardic's body temperature had to be above 98.6. Heat emanated off her exposed skin, and during a brief moment of insanity, Olivia glanced over at the strong column of Cardic's neck. Olivia could feel herself begin to salivate.

With Cardic still this close to her, Olivia found it difficult to remember why this was a bad idea. She swallowed to give her a moment to catch her breath. "No. No, nothing. You'll have to find someone else to take home tonight." Olivia hoped the insult sounded as harsh as she'd intended and not as breathless as she felt.

"Patience is a virtue."

"As is avoidance," Olivia grumbled. With Cardic even just a few more inches away from her, she could think more clearly.

"And persistence. I'll be in touch. Olivia."

Her name was said with just enough emphasis and sexual promise that Olivia felt herself almost blush. Almost. *Olivia Reynolds does not blush.*

As she watched her walk away, Olivia was disturbed to note Cardic's backside was just as impressive as her front.

Chapter Six

Olivia listened as Vivian droned on about catalog orders, displays, and meeting dates but couldn't pull her eyes away from the window. Her office window was level with the tracks of the Pink Line train, and today the rumble of the train passing by every few minutes was less soothing and more irritating. For a moment, she felt relieved it was Friday until she remembered she only had three weeks until her brand overview report was due to the president of Vital, so weekends would be nonexistent until then. At least when she came in on Saturdays, she was usually alone.

She spun her chair around to face Vivian and vowed to be more focused for what remained of her day. "I'm sorry, Vivian, can you repeat that last part?"

Vivian stopped writing and looked up at Olivia like a deer in headlights. "Repeat?"

"Is there a problem?" Olivia sensed that Vivian was just surprised at her lack of focus, so she added an extra note of authority to her voice that she usually reserved for the marketing team or the idiots from the design department.

"No, no, ma'am. No problem. You've just never asked me to repeat myself."

"Well, I'm asking you now. What did you say about Melissa?"

As the head designer for the women's athletic wear department for Vital, Melissa was an integral part of the success of the spring line, especially with the additions Olivia had proposed since her promotion. Melissa was young, talented, beautiful, and a complete snob. On more than one occasion, Olivia got the feeling that Melissa didn't see any need for plus-size athletic wear. Melissa must have been around a size two and even referred to the new line as "hippo wear."

"I was just saying Melissa has requested a meeting with you. She said it's urgent. I put her down for Thursday at nine thirty, so I had to move your conference call with the buyer from Bloomingdale's to eleven."

Olivia picked up her brain stress ball and thought hard about the bottle of wine chilling in her fridge. *Maybe I can get out of here by eight.*

"Did she say what it was regarding?"

"She said the team was running into an issue with the fit of the racerback sports bra, but she'd go into more detail with you."

Olivia suppressed a groan. She and Melissa had talked at length three weeks ago about the racerback sports bra, and Melissa's specific complaint that it didn't provide enough support for "well-endowed" women. *Idiot.* Olivia had been wearing the sample the team made in her size for the past two months. She'd actually been wearing it when she met Cardic.

Olivia didn't know whether to be pleased or concerned that the resentment coursing through her veins a moment ago was replaced with an almost relaxed feeling when she thought of Cardic and remembered her hair ruffling in the lake breeze. At least thinking about Cardic would let her forget momentarily about Melissa and her incompetent bitchiness.

Cardic's persistence the Saturday before had been flattering, but Olivia was sure, really sure this time, that they would never see each other again. For the best. Even though there was something sexy and dapper about the woman who had almost given her a concussion.

"Boss. You okay? I've never seen you look so serene when we talk about Melissa," Vivian said, putting her pencil in her hair and rising from her chair, not waiting for a reply.

"Maybe I'm turning over a new leaf. I'll be here for a least another few hours going over the marketing presentation, but you go ahead and get out of here at five."

"Will do. I have to finish the data pull from last spring's sales, then I'm gone. Have a good one."

Two hours later, Olivia sat adding her final notes to the marketing deck. Pleased with the presentation, she saved her notes and packed up. Her office phone rang, and Olivia grabbed it, figuring it was Vivian.

"I'm still here. Did you forget something?"

"Yeah, to ask you for your number. But Joan was kind enough to provide me with your last name. Still not sure if it was intentional or not."

Olivia's senses were automatically on high alert at the sound of Cardic's voice and the knowledge that she had gone to the trouble of tracking her down. As the slight excitement died down, her annoyance grew. How could Cardic sound so casual when she had most likely just Internet stalked Olivia to get her number?

"Are you stalking me?" Olivia put down her bag and slumped in her chair, suddenly feeling exhausted.

"Not stalking. Researching," Cardic said, her voice calm and even. "Impressive résumé, Ms. Reynolds. I must tell you I love Vital's cleats. I wore them all through college."

"Let me guess. Softball?"

"Soccer." Olivia could hear the sexy smile in Cardic's voice. "So, dinner?"

"No."

"No?" Cardic sounded surprised and almost offended, as if the trouble she went through to Google Olivia was reason enough for her to say yes.

"No. It's an adverb. In this case expressing refusal. Are you unfamiliar with the word?"

"As a matter of fact, I am. Are you still mad I knocked you over, or that I don't put my dog on a leash?"

Olivia smirked, remembering the shaggy creature that had licked her entire face before she could stand up. "Neither. I'm just busy. And you're not my type."

"What? Sexy, intelligent, and successful?"

"Cocky, clumsy, and controlling," Olivia spat out without thinking, more irritated by the second. How could she possibly have had any positive response to a phone call from this egomaniac?

"Controlling? Just go to dinner with me, and if you don't have a good time, I swear I'll leave you alone."

The deal sounded fair enough and almost too good to be true. There's no way Olivia would enjoy an evening in Cardic's company. And if she didn't, maybe Cardic would stay true to her word and leave her the hell alone. "Fine. I should have some time Thursday evening."

Cardic pumped her fist, realizing she felt like a freshman who just got a yes from the homecoming queen.

"So, I'll pick you up around seven?"

The silence on the other end of the line made Cardic wonder if Olivia had changed her mind.

"No, I'll pick you up."

Cardic had no qualms about not being the one driving, so she rattled off her address and said good night. Olivia's earlier comment about Cardic being controlling popped into her mind. Cardic knew she needed to tread lightly, so she resisted the urge to name a restaurant or suggest they take a walk by the lake after dinner. She'd give Olivia as much control as she needed as long as she got to see her again.

Cardic glanced at the clock before continuing the family tree document on the Yanapo. Since there was an absence of monogamy, and the women were often sexually active with more than one man, trying to determine paternity was futile. Cardic had dozens of handwritten notes from interviews she conducted with the tribe's people. Out of thirty-one women of childbearing age, only two had felt certain who the fathers of their children were. In their culture, as long as a woman produced a healthy baby, there was little to no value placed on paternity.

Cardic rubbed her eyes with the heels of her hands and wondered what life would be like if people felt no need to latch on to a certain person above all others. On more than one occasion since they met, Cardic had to laugh at herself about this need to see Olivia again. She was one of the sexiest, most fascinating women Cardic had met in months, maybe years. Of course, there was no other cosmic, fated reason. But she knew how it might look to someone like her sister Claire, who believed in love and happy endings. Cardic and Olivia's happy ending would come as soon as things fizzled out in the bedroom, then they'd go their separate ways. Which was fine with Cardic. Maybe when she got the redheaded siren out of her system, she could fully concentrate on her data.

Once she finished with the digital family tree, she'd begin tacking the photos to the wall and arranging them for a visual display that was easily accessible. Or Patrick would begin tacking the photos to the wall. Patrick, a digital native, would have no trouble opening up and navigating a document every time he needed info, but Cardic needed the faces of these people right in front of her. She needed to be able to look from one face to another without worrying about scrolling or clicking. Even tiny actions like these would take away valuable think time.

"Okay. Let's keep the momentum," Cardic said to herself as she pulled out another info card. "Ah, Yako."

Yako ended up being one of her favorite people during her study. He was patient with her learning their language; he answered any questions she had, going into as much detail as she needed; and he was one of the few people present during her tattoo ceremony. He had an incredible outlook on life and relationships with his tribesmen.

Cardic flipped the card over to look at Yako's young, masculine face. Like many of the Yanapo men, Yako kept his face clean-shaven except for a very small growth of hair above his lip. He had the traditional adult man's haircut of their culture, a short-cropped bowl cut. The most striking and memorable thing about Yako, however, was his eyes. A bright hazel, almost yellow in color. Cardic had never seen anyone with eyes that color, especially not in an Amazonian culture.

At almost eleven o'clock, Cardic saved the work on her laptop and packed up. Tempted to stop at one of her favorite bars on the way home for a drink and maybe some female company, Cardic thought better of it as she turned out the lights and locked her office door. A tremor of arousal had run through her body just hearing Olivia's voice. A few moments with a willing stranger would take the edge off. The idea was tempting, but the next time she had sex it would be with Olivia, if all went according to plan. The memory of her smooth, curvy body popped to mind. Oh, she could definitely wait until Thursday.

CHAPTER SEVEN

Yes, Mr. McKinnon. I will have the presentation to you by this afternoon. Yes, thank you." Olivia hung up the phone and opened her email, pulling up the deck Roger from the marketing team sent her yesterday.

"I need Roger in here today. Before lunch."

"Sure, Boss. I'll call down to marketing now. Anything else you need?" Vivian asked from just outside Olivia's office. With things this busy, Olivia had been leaving her office door open to more easily get hold of Vivian if she needed her.

Olivia scrolled through the deck and was pleased to see all the changes she had suggested were in place, along with a few improvements she hadn't even thought of. *Exquisite.* And as she and Roger had discussed, there were several plus-size models now intermixed in the proposed advertisements.

With a smile, Olivia pushed back from her desk and glanced out her window. People milling about below were wearing sweaters and light coats. The chill of fall was near, and Olivia couldn't wait. Something about the fall seemed so hopeful and productive. The heat in Chicago during the summer was oppressive and irritating. *Irritating. Like Cardic.*

With their Thursday dinner date only two days away, Olivia found her focus wavering. Twice this morning she'd picked up the phone to call Cardic and cancel, then realized she didn't even have her number. Or last name.

"Roger said he'd be up in ten minutes. He sounded horrified. The deck look okay?"

"Horrified?" Olivia turned to look at Vivian, who had rolled her chair in front of Olivia's door. The idea that she could horrify anyone was both welcome and unsettling. Olivia knew scaring people into doing what she needed was effective, and she'd been perfecting the art since coming into the corporate world, but at the same time, she felt saddened to think she was the kind of person people avoided in the break room and hoped didn't attend the staff Christmas party. "Am I that scary?"

Vivian's face registered something close to shock, then softened. "Well, no. But we all know what high expectations you have for this project. Roger has been working hard. I guess he's just nervous."

The phone ringing pulled Vivian from the doorway, and Olivia turned her attention back to the marketing presentation.

"Joan on line two," Olivia heard Vivian call.

As she picked up the phone and held it with her shoulder, Olivia reached into her mini fridge for a bottle of water.

"Joanie, what's up? Don't cancel on me tonight. I'm leaving early to cook you dinner."

"Not a chance. Just calling to make sure you weren't working yourself to the bone tonight. Need me to bring something? Wine?"

"Red would be good."

"You got it. Also, I just got free tickets to the White Sox rivalry game for this Saturday, but I've got that gig at Fox and Hound. You want them?"

"Yes, of course! Are you sure there's no way you can't reschedule?" Olivia and Joan hadn't been to a rivalry game in years. Since they were both from the South Side of Chicago, being die-hard Sox fans was as natural as breathing.

"No, I've been dying to play Fox and Hound. Maybe next game?"

"Ugh, fine. See you in a few."

Olivia pulled up a new browser tab to search the schedule and find out what time the game started on Saturday. A knock on the doorframe pulled her attention from the screen.

A nervous-looking Roger stood shuffling his feet, waiting for her to invite him in.

"Roger, please come in. Have a seat."

"Olivia, I hope everything looks okay. I addressed the changes you suggested and made a few others." Roger pulled out a printed copy of the deck and slid it across Olivia's desk as he sat down, pulling at his collar.

Olivia pushed the document back to him and leaned back in her chair. "Roger, I think—"

"Are the graphics on page seven still too small? I want them to be readable, but any bigger, and we'll need an extra page, and I know you said to be concise." He quickly flipped through the deck to find the page in question.

"No, no, Roger. I think it looks great. And I love the changes you made. It's perfect."

His relieved smile made Olivia realize praise wasn't something he was used to getting from her. One of her favorite professors in school always reminded her to recognize hard work, and since her promotion, she was in a position where it was critical for her to be honest with her feedback. *Credit where credit is due.*

"Really, Roger," she continued, "it looks great. I'm sending it over to McKinnon today, and I just wanted to thank you and your team for all your hard work." The statement was unfamiliar but not unpleasant to say out loud.

"Thanks, Olivia. I'll let them know. Thanks," he said again before excusing himself.

Later that night as Olivia put the final touch of oregano in her grandmother's pasta sauce, she thought again about her impending date with Cardic. Neither of them had suggested a restaurant, so she wasn't sure what to wear. She'd ask Joan but wasn't even sure yet if she wanted to tell her about the date. It'd be better to just tell her after it turned out to be a complete failure and waste of her time—that way Joan wouldn't get her hopes up. "Hopes up for what?" Olivia snorted as she pulled two wineglasses from the dishwasher and placed them on the island.

Just as Olivia placed the garlic bread in the oven, she heard Joan walk through the door.

"Parking in this neighborhood is such a bitch! I can't believe you moved up here. Sellout," Joan said as she placed the wine on the counter and kissed Olivia's cheek.

"It's closer to work. And I'm not a sellout. Dad still lives on the South Side, and I'm there all the time." After her second year at Vital, Olivia decided to buy a small condo in Old Town since it would be closer to work, and also to get some independence from her dad. George Reynolds knew Olivia was capable of accomplishing anything on her own but was still a helicopter dad at times. Olivia often thought it was more for his own benefit than for hers.

The building was vintage and small for the area, only four floors and sixteen units. Most condos on this street were high-rises with views of the lake. When apartment hunting, Olivia had learned the term "vintage charm" just meant old. After six months of looking at apartments, she wasn't thrilled when her Realtor lined this one up, but really the only thing old about this building was the outside and the beautiful crown molding and wainscoting throughout the entire apartment. Everything else had been updated. New energy efficient windows, stainless steel appliances, and white quartz countertops. A large spa-like shower with double showerheads was also a rare find for a building built in the thirties.

The selling point for Olivia was the sunroom, or what the Realtor referred to as the "conservatory." Measuring six by five feet, it was small but had a great view of the quiet street below, and Olivia spent most of her spare time there. Not that she had much. She'd been gifted two black thumbs from her mother, so unlike what the room might have been intended for, there were no plants. Instead, the tiny room housed her favorite books, framed pictures, and candles. It was the only place in her home that had any sort of personal touches. She'd spent a few months cultivating furniture and art for her apartment, but it was all very functional and impersonal, similar to many of the staged apartments she had walked through.

"So, how's work? Great, I'm sure," Joan said as she poured a nearly overflowing glass of wine for herself and a normal glass for Olivia.

"Slow down, cowboy. Work okay for you?" Olivia put her glass down and piled plates with pasta, meatballs, and garlic bread.

"Yeah, yeah, it's fine. Just wish I could quit my day job and do what I really want to do. Not all of us were lucky enough to find our dream career right out of college."

"I'm very fortunate. I wish you could just do what you love. I can't imagine how frustrating it is. But the booze cruise went really well, huh?" As soon as the words left her mouth, Olivia regretted them. Only even a slight reference to that evening and Joan would jump at the chance to ask about Cardic.

Joan's eyes widened, and she put down her glass after a healthy sip, winding pasta around her fork. "I let your last name slip, but my break was over before I could accidentally give her your number. I figured she is smart enough to find you. Have you heard from the good doctor?" Joan lifted a heaping forkful of pasta to her mouth and leaned over her plate.

Olivia's head snapped up. "Doctor?" Olivia was the furthest thing from a gold digger, but being raised and abandoned by one at a young age, certain words registered quickly with the brain. All the word *doctor* meant to Olivia was that the woman must in some way be intelligent, hardworking, and serious. None of the characteristics she would equate with Cardic based on their first few meetings. "Doctor of what?"

Joan put down her fork, crossed her arms, and beamed triumphantly. Olivia studied her own pasta and realized her question implied she had some interest in Cardic. "Don't give me that look. I don't care. She just didn't strike me as a doctor, that's all."

"Yeah, whatever. It's *Doctor* Cardic Lawson. Professor of anthropology at Loyola. She's thirty-six. Don't you like older women?"

"That's only four years. And you learned all this from a thirty-second dance with her?"

"I was trying to get intel. And you're deflecting. Did she call you or not?"

"She did. We have a date, what I'm positive will only be *one* date, on Thursday. It's just to make you happy and get her to leave me the hell alone. And I don't want to hear anything about it." Olivia pinned Joan with a stare, and when she didn't respond, went back to eating her pasta. Leaving the meatballs, Olivia took her plate to the sink, assuring herself the flutter in her stomach was due to too much Parmesan cheese and nothing to do with Dr. Cardic Lawson.

❖

"So you see, in the Yanomami culture, polygamy is quite common. There are men with many wives, and the violence inside a tribe is often related to sexual jealousy between two men vying for the same woman." Cardic emphasized this point by drawing hearts around the crude stick figures she'd drawn on the whiteboard.

Shannon, an intelligent and outgoing freshman, raised her hand and didn't wait to be called on before she spoke. "But the women don't have more than one husband?"

"Not within this tribe, no." Cardic looked around to gauge the reaction of her mostly female class. In the last two years, she had added an extra day to this lesson just for discussion purposes based on the interest, and sometimes outrage, of the class when they learned about the conditions women suffered in this tribe at the hands of their husbands. "Now, as I mentioned last week, a large part of your grade this semester is your term paper comparing two tribes in one cultural area. To give you an idea what I'm looking for, let's compare the Yanomami to the tribe I did fieldwork with last year, the Yanapo."

A frat boy who always chose to sit in the back of the classroom spoke up. "You said they don't get married."

"Bingo. What a perfect place to start. Thank you, Mr. Kennedy." Cardic tried not to embarrass the kid too much. Although his comment was obvious, at least he was attempting to participate. "Now, while the Yanomami don't have a set ritual for marriage, it varies from tribe to tribe; marriage is a social construct within the culture. The Yanapo, on the other hand, have no marriage ritual and it is socially acceptable for men and women within the tribe, who are of age, to have as many sexual partners as they wish. The men and women alike have sexual freedom."

Cardic glanced again at her class as they took notes and digested the information she spewed at them. At times she wished she could somehow transport her students to the jungle so they could feel the energy and passion of the people she spoke of. Hearing her drone on for an hour was surely not as inspiring. The faces and names of all the tribespeople flashed through her mind. Although she'd conducted dozens of hours of interviews with the tribe's people, most things she'd learned from being completely immersed in the culture.

When most of the students had finished writing and their attention was back on her, she posed a simple question, "What implications does this have on the culture? On the women? On the interpersonal relationships within the tribe itself?"

After a lively discussion with her students, Cardic dismissed the class and packed up. It was almost five o'clock so she didn't have long to check in with Patrick upstairs, then go home to get ready for her date with Olivia.

Agonizing over data, grading papers, and teaching four classes a week was keeping her busy but still couldn't keep her mind off Olivia. Cardic didn't know what their date would be like; they hadn't even discussed where they'd be going. Usually, her dates were a polite excuse to get a woman into bed, but something about Olivia screamed restraint, as if Cardic might be chipping away at an ice block for days. An image of Olivia lying naked on her bed, bathed in candlelight, as Cardic rubbed an ice cube down her abdomen popped into her head. If she had to guess, chipping away at the ice would be well worth it.

Chapter Eight

Olivia pulled her Lexus into a space about a block away from Cardic's apartment. Her Realtor had shown her several condos in this area. The neighborhood of Lincoln Park was a nice mix of young families and urban professionals, but a few too many college kids for Olivia's taste.

Olivia locked her car, then straightened her skirt before heading down the street. She glanced at the street signs to make sure she wouldn't get a ticket for where she'd decided to park. She'd changed outfits six times before finally settling on a mid-length wool skirt, a sheer black top, and her favorite black blazer. If she felt too overdressed, she could always leave her blazer in the car. Her heels clicked loudly on the sidewalk as she quickened her pace. Olivia hated to be late, and she was ready to get this date over and done.

Turning down Cardic's street, Olivia was surprised at the number of trees that flanked both sides of the one-way street. Olivia imagined the trees ablaze with brilliant reds, yellows, and oranges once the leaves began to change. Many of the homes appeared to be flats, with separate apartments on each floor.

As Olivia approached the address Cardic had given her, she noted the small but well-kept yard in the front and the twisting vines clinging to the bricks and window frames. It was a gorgeous building. Olivia studied the three-story structure and wondered which floor Cardic lived on.

She headed to the steps, then saw the front door open before she could reach the porch.

Cardic stood there in bare feet and baggy jeans with that knowing grin on her face. Her Loyola T-shirt was too big but not unflattering. It did nothing to hide the subtle swell of her breasts, and the curve of her biceps was visible under the short sleeves. Olivia's mouth watered. *How can she look that good when it looks like she just crawled out of bed?* Olivia didn't care about skin tone one way or another, but something was striking about Cardic's bronzed arms against the stark white of her T-shirt.

Olivia grasped at anger and ignored her racing pulse as she stared at Cardic's attire and gestured to her bare feet. "Are we going to a sports bar? You'll have to at least put on shoes."

Before Olivia could hear what she assumed was going to be a smart-ass reply, Cicero bounded down the steps to greet her with Cardic chasing behind.

"Cicero, go back inside." The dog obeyed before he could paw at Olivia's skirt.

Cardic walked closer to Olivia and looked her up and down. "We don't have to go anywhere." Her tone was sultry and deep. Again, Olivia felt herself grow warm. Cockiness was not something she usually found attractive in a woman, but on Cardic it seemed to fit.

"Well, I'm hungry."

Staring at her mouth, Cardic said, "Me too." She was close enough that Olivia could smell her. A subtle, clean smell but hard to define. "Come on up. I'm almost ready."

I'm ready now. Olivia thought, trying not to stare at Cardic's ass as she took the steps two at a time.

Cardic's third-floor apartment was bigger than Olivia would've thought from the street. There were two large brown leather sofas flanking the bay window and a low coffee table covered with papers and file folders. To the right of the entrance was a dining room table, but it was hard to tell because it was covered with large boxes and more files. Bookshelves lined every open wall, and there was a large oil painting of the Chicago skyline hanging above the fireplace. The kitchen was sparsely furnished with stainless steel appliances, the granite countertop littered with mail and magazines.

"Make yourself at home. I just need to change." Cardic backed toward a narrow hallway leading to what Olivia assumed was the bedroom. "Sorry about all the files. Would you like a drink?"

"No, I'm fine. Thank you."

"Great. I'll be right out."

As Cicero curled up on a comfy dog bed on the floor, Olivia glanced at a group of framed pictures on a table beside the sofa. One was of a gorgeous little boy who had Cardic's deep brown eyes and unruly hair. Another picture of the child showed him holding a rubber ducky and laughing in a bubble bath. The next, a larger picture, was of Cardic with her arm around a beautiful woman. She too had the deep brown eyes, and Olivia assumed it must be her sister. Cardic looked much younger in the picture but just as carefree and sexy.

"My sister Claire and her son Clark," Cardic said from somewhere behind her.

"They're beautiful." Olivia turned around to find Cardic dressed in a pair of perfectly fitted black slacks and a plain white oxford shirt. Olivia caught a peek of the elastic of Cardic's underwear as she tucked in her shirt. At that moment, she couldn't recall ever seeing something so mouthwatering. She scolded herself for the juvenile and hormonal response to Cardic's body like she'd never seen an attractive woman before.

"Thanks. People say we look alike."

"Does modesty run in the family, too?"

"Not in the least. You're driving, so did you want to pick a restaurant?"

Olivia stared for a moment. Other than caressing every inch of Olivia with her eyes in the front yard, Cardic seemed rather blasé about the evening. Maybe she was dreading it the way Olivia had been all week. *You wouldn't have changed that many times if you were dreading it.* "I know a great Mexican place in Pilsen, right off Eighteenth Avenue. The pineapple pomegranate guacamole is to die for."

When Cardic didn't respond, Olivia headed toward the door, but Cardic caught her by the hand and turned her around. They stood only a few inches apart, and Olivia tried to keep her breathing normal.

"Your hair looks gorgeous this way." Cardic twirled a wavy strand around her finger and stared into Olivia's eyes.

Maybe not so blasé. "You've only seen me twice before." Olivia made an effort to sound normal.

"I liked your hair then, too. I don't want to come on too strong, but I'm tied up in knots here."

It took everything in Cardic not to grab Olivia by the shoulders and kiss her right then and there. She'd give Olivia control, if it didn't kill her first. When she saw Olivia walk up the sidewalk in her body-fitting skirt and a sheer black top that tastefully showcased the black bra beneath, Cardic's heart almost stopped. She'd spent six hours being perfectly still, hunting small game in the jungle, with bugs crawling on her face and sweat dripping in her eyes, but for the life of her, Cardic could not figure out how she was going to survive the evening without begging Olivia to put her out of her misery.

Sex for Cardic was enjoyable and relaxing, but waiting for it had never been her strong suit. Of course, if her partner liked to draw things out she'd accommodate them, but her own release came quick and hard with very little buildup.

There was an almost imperceptible change in Olivia's breathing as Cardic tugged gently on the strand of fiery red hair. That was encouragement enough.

The restaurant Olivia had chosen was dimly lit and not very crowded. At the garden level of a vintage building, it held an old-fashioned romantic quality, and for a moment, Cardic wondered why Olivia had chosen a restaurant so intimate since she'd been hesitant to even have dinner. Perhaps the ambience would work in Cardic's favor. She'd yet to consider what Olivia's reaction would be to the tricks she had up her sleeve. The round tables were covered in linen tablecloths, with small vases, each holding one pink rose. The hostess greeted Olivia by name and lead them to a candlelit table by the front window.

While the server droned on about the specials, Cardic took pleasure in watching Olivia unawares. Her green eyes tracked the menu items from beneath thick black lashes. Her eye makeup was what Cardic understood to be "smoky" and her lips shined with a deep red tone. It occurred to Cardic at that moment, she'd very much like to see Olivia with no makeup. *And no clothes.*

"And for you?" The server interrupted the turn her thoughts had taken.

Cardic glanced down at the menu for the first time and picked something familiar. After folding her menu, she handed it back to the server.

"So you're a doctor?" Olivia said with a teasing smile. "My mother would be so proud of me."

Cardic held up her hands and laughed out loud. "Not a

brain surgeon. Doctorate in cultural anthropology. I teach the undergrad anthropology courses at Loyola."

"And do you specialize in one area?"

"Polygamy. Marital customs. The study of monogamy, actually. Or lack thereof." Cardic held Olivia's gaze, watching the soft light play across her eyes.

"Lack? Are there any cultures that aren't monogamous?" Olivia leaned back as the server brought their margaritas.

"Not many. I just returned from a field study of the Yanapo. They're quite the anomaly. All the surrounding tribes in the Amazon have polygamy practices." Cardic refrained from saying more, not sure if Olivia was genuinely interested or just being polite.

"Wow. How long were you in the Amazon?" Olivia sipped her margarita and stirred it with a small straw. Her hands were even sexy. She had long fingers with dark polish and a silver ring on her right hand. The stone appeared to be an opal.

Cardic took a sip of her own margarita and tried to concentrate on the conversation. "A little over eighteen months. It was a great experience. Life-changing."

"What was the best part?"

Cardic hesitated. The best part? She'd been asked a million questions about her experience. What she learned, if she would go back, implications on her instruction and writing an ethnography. No one, not even her sister, had asked her what she had enjoyed the most about the experience. It was work after all, not leisure. "It was, I guess…well, when I got there I was an observer. It felt very technical. Very detached. But by the time I left, it was like leaving family behind." Cardic absentmindedly rubbed her now-healed tattoo. She knew it took anthropologists time to readjust to life after leaving a field study, but nothing had prepared her for the mourning and feeling of loss when she returned home. Attempting to avoid any more time reflecting on the still raw and emotional experience, Cardic changed the subject. "And what about you? What do you enjoy most about working for Vital?"

"I'm an expert in avoidance, Dr. Lawson. You aren't fooling anyone." Olivia delivered the barb with a sexy smile that made her lips shine in the soft light. Cardic didn't mind being scolded when it came from that mouth. "My work for Vital. It's challenging. I'm always up for a challenge. Right now we are getting ready to launch the new fall line, which for the first time in Vital's history will include plus-size sportswear. With the body positive movement, it's important we stay on trend. And with the average women in the U.S. at a size sixteen, we'd be losing a lot of customers and a lot of money without that inclusivity."

"But it's not all about the money."

It was Olivia's turn to hesitate. Cardic wondered for a moment if she would even respond.

"No. As a plus-size woman myself, it's important to me that all women be represented by Vital."

"Plus-size. What does that mean exactly? I just buy clothes that fit. I buy stuff without trying it on or even looking at the tag."

"Well, strictly speaking, plus-size is a size twelve or above. I doubt you've ever fit into a twelve in your life with a build like yours."

"You noticed my build, Ms. Reynolds?" Cardic felt her blood rush hot as Olivia's eyes moved down her face and throat to settle on her breasts.

"I noticed you aren't plus-sized. The top complaint from women sizes twelve or above is what we affectionately refer to as skinny privilege. Being able to walk into Gap or Hollister and buy a pair of jeans."

Cardic felt like a fifteen-year-old. Olivia couldn't even

discuss her career without Cardic imagining taking her out of a pair of jeans.

"Of course, there are plenty of great plus-size designers, but for the average plus-size woman, finding those designers or affording clothes from specialty plus-size websites isn't practical."

"And I'm assuming, like myself, you're married to your job and have time for little else."

"Precisely." Olivia felt relieved Cardic seemed to be getting the hint that whatever she had in mind for the two of them was just not on Olivia's radar. "I really don't have time for any sort of relationship. Or desire for one. Working seventy hours a week, most weekends, and odd hours doesn't leave room for any sort of romantic obligations."

"I can imagine. I'm not one for romance either."

As the waitress set down their plates, Olivia felt nervous, like Cardic was buttering her up for something. "So we're on the same page, then?"

"About romantic relationships? Absolutely. I guess I failed to mention I study monogamy because of my belief that it's an antiquated, unnatural social construct."

"I see." This hit Olivia like a ton of bricks. So Cardic wasn't looking for a quick, torrid romance? At the twinge of disappointment that she wasn't the object of Cardic's desire and would no longer be turning her away repeatedly, Olivia continued. "So then why did you ask me to dinner? Over and over? If you don't even see yourself in a relationship with someone?"

"Not a romantic, monogamous relationship, no. To be honest, Olivia, I want you so bad I can't see straight. Thoughts of you are distracting me, and my body is on fire any time I picture you in that skimpy running shirt you had on when we met. I'd like us to enter into an arrangement that would make that possible."

"Skimpy? It was not skimpy. And what sort of arrangement did you have in mind?" Olivia put her fork down and folded her napkin over her plate, suddenly done with her meal.

"A sexual arrangement. I realize we're both busy, so scheduling will be the most difficult aspect, but we can play it any way you want. You can be in control. You call the shots."

The blasé attitude of earlier in the evening had returned, and Olivia gritted her teeth as Cardic draped her arm over the back of the booth. Not a care in the world. Her frame stretched out and posture relaxed. She didn't look at all like a woman who had just suggested a sexual fling. She resembled some languid jungle cat, relaxing in a tree, confident her prey would come close enough for her to pounce without much work required.

Olivia tried to control her rising temper and keep her voice down in the quiet restaurant. She bit her bottom lip for a moment before replying. "I'm sorry, did I give you the impression that I was for hire? That I would just lay out a red carpet for you?"

"I meant no offense. After hearing you're just as married to your job as I am, I thought you'd be interested." Cardic did look surprised. Which annoyed Olivia even more.

"And what made you think that?"

"The way you're looking at me. Right now. Yeah, I know you're pissed, but there's heat here. You can't deny that."

Olivia opened her mouth to respond, then shut it again. She was nothing if not honest. Especially with herself. Of course there was heat. It didn't mean there had to be anything else. "I'm not denying it. I'm simply saying it doesn't mean I want to sleep with you."

Cardic leaned forward and stared into Olivia's eyes. She licked her lips. Something Olivia noticed she did quite a lot. Unconsciously and often. It wasn't crude. It was sexy.

Olivia took time to rake her eyes over Cardic's face. Her dark eyes screamed with the promise of pleasure, and those full lips made Olivia ache to kiss her. *Damn it.*

"Olivia. It would be so good between us. What is your objection?"

Cardic leaned away to let the server put the bill down and clear their plates, and Olivia took a breath and held it for a moment, trying to conjure up from thin air some excuse as to why she didn't want to sleep with Cardic. All the lies she'd told herself were not convincing. When had this evening taken such a strange turn?

After Cardic paid the bill, she grabbed Olivia's jacket from the coat hook near the door and held it out for her. Olivia slid her arms into the sleeves and almost gasped when Cardic's warm fingers brushed the nape of her neck. As she leaned forward, Cardic's breath fanned her ear. "I have an idea."

They exited the restaurant and headed down Racine Avenue toward Olivia's car. Curiosity got the best of her. "You said you had an idea?"

"I have your interest now, do I?" Cardic slowed to a stroll and turned down a small alley. She stopped and leaned against the brick wall. Olivia envied the ease with which Cardic seemed to do everything. Walking, talking, sitting, leaning. *Propositioning people for sex.*

Cardic grabbed Olivia's hand and pulled her closer. It wasn't a demand; it was a request that Olivia's body gladly granted.

"Well?" Olivia was growing more irritated by the second, while at the same time her body hummed with arousal.

"Kiss me." Cardic licked her lips, and Olivia caught the barest hint of a smile.

Arrogant little shit. With renewed annoyance, Olivia decided to show Cardic exactly how unaffected she was by the heat between them.

Olivia grabbed the nape of Cardic's neck and stepped between her spread thighs. She moved close to Cardic's face and glanced down at her full lips. Cardic exhaled, and Olivia could feel the warmth of her breath against her lips. As she moved closer, Olivia pressed her lips to Cardic's.

Cardic palmed Olivia's hips and pulled her closer as their lips brushed. Olivia tried not to moan at the contact. It had been a while since she'd slept with someone, and the warmth of Cardic's mouth and body set her on fire. Her nipples hardened, and her stomach clenched.

A moment ago, Cardic had been relaxed and casual, but now as Olivia ran her hands under the neck of Cardic's shirt, her muscles bunched with sexual tension. Cardic continued to pull and grab at Olivia's hips, trying to pull her closer.

Olivia enjoyed Cardic's response, and she grew bolder. As she ran her hands through Cardic's hair, she slipped her tongue into Cardic's mouth.

As their kiss deepened, Cardic slid one of her hands up to cup Olivia's breast. Her nipples had always been sensitive, but as Cardic's thumb traced the hardened peak, Olivia pulled her mouth away to catch her breath.

Of their own accord, Olivia's hips moved, trying to answer the heady rush of desire flowing through her veins and settling in her groin.

Cardic bent forward and attacked Olivia's neck with gentle nips and bites. "Come home with me."

Olivia waited a moment to reply. She moved her neck

away from Cardic's distracting mouth and glanced into her coffee eyes. "I thought I was calling the shots?"

"Is that a yes?"

Before Olivia could answer, Cardic's phone rang in her pocket. Cardic didn't even glance down, keeping her eyes on Olivia's, letting her gaze roam over Olivia's neck and breasts every few seconds.

"You were saying?" Cardic tucked an errant strand of hair behind Olivia's ear.

"I think—"

When Cardic's phone rang again, she muttered a curse and pulled it out of her pocket. Cardic glanced at the display, and Olivia guessed it was important since Cardic stepped out of her reach and faced the wall.

As gut-wrenching as it felt to have Cardic move away from her, it at least gave her a moment to think. Olivia wiped the moisture from her bottom lip and realized how juvenile this whole scene was. Standing in an alleyway making out with a near stranger.

After a muffled conversation, Cardic turned around with a solemn look on her face.

"I'm sorry. It's my sister. I've gotta go. She's on her way to the hospital with my nephew."

Olivia remembered the brown-eyed boy from the photos in Cardic's apartment. Olivia hoped the boy was all right but took it as a sign from the universe that this was not going to happen. No matter how amazing Cardic tasted or how delicious and hard her body felt.

"Is everything okay?"

"A high fever. My sister's kind of a worrier. But she's going through a bad divorce right now—"

"No, I understand. Do you need a ride?"

"It's out of your way. I'll just catch a cab. But this isn't over, Olivia."

Cardic pulled Olivia into her arms and kissed her roughly on the mouth.

As they walked slowly back to the sidewalk and Cardic hailed a cab, Olivia wondered what the best words would be to decline Cardic's offer of a no-strings sexual arrangement.

Chapter Nine

The emergency room at St. Joseph's hospital was not the most crowded Cardic had ever seen. As she glanced around for her sister, Cardic realized the last time she'd been here had been for a broken nose. An elbow to the face during soccer practice. She'd never forget the metallic smell of blood.

"Cardic," Claire called from the other side of the waiting room, "we're over here."

Claire was sitting in one of the standard waiting room chairs, with a sleeping Clark resting his head on her shoulder. Wearing a roomy gray sweater and baggy jeans, her hair pulled into a messy ponytail, she was dressed like a college kid studying for finals. But a closer look at her weary face and Cardic realized she looked more her age than she ever had.

Cardic kissed her cheek and rubbed Clark's back, noting his damp forehead and red face. "Why haven't they taken you back yet?" Anger churned in Cardic's belly, replacing the warm tickle that had settled there during her make-out session with Olivia.

"I don't know. No room, I guess."

"Wait here." Cardic glanced at the triage nurse and smiled.

The woman looked to be about thirty-five and had a kind face. There was a fifty-fifty chance she'd be offended at being flirted with by a woman, but Cardic would take her chances.

"Hey, there."

The woman looked up from her computer screen and studied Cardic's face and what she could see of her body over the tall counter. Cardic assumed she liked what she saw, as a sly smile spread across her face. "Can I help you, doll?"

"Yes," Cardic paused and made a show of glancing at the woman's chest to read her name tag, "Mary, you can. That's my sister and nephew over there. They'd be much more comfortable in a room. Is there anything you can do for me?"

Mary giggled. "Not anything my husband would like." She winked as she looked down at a clipboard. "But I think I can help your nephew. Come on back."

The wait for the doctor seemed endless, and Cardic paced instead of cursing. Looking at Clark, small and fragile, in the hospital bed made her feel helpless. "Where the hell is the doctor? And where the hell is your husband?"

"Ex," Claire replied calmly, "and he's in Arizona with his new in-laws. Will you stop pacing? You're acting like Dad."

Cardic stopped in her tracks and leaned against the door instead. Any action that reminded Claire, or anyone, of her father would not be continued if she could help it. Instead, Cardic knocked her head lightly against the door. Claire walked over and hugged her.

"I didn't mean that." After patting her cheek, Claire went back to Clark's bedside. "Tell me what they did for fevers in the jungle."

A deep calm rushed Cardic's inside as it always did when she remembered the Yanapo. "If the shaman decided you weren't possessed, then the elder women would boil local plants and grind them up to make a paste. That's applied to the chest of the sick person. They used it on me once. It was very soothing."

Cardic again studied her sister's solemn face. She didn't mind supporting Claire in anything and would always be there for her, but she couldn't imagine how many times in a day Claire wished she had a loving and supportive spouse—the one she thought she'd had when she married David.

After a two-hour wait and the ungodly experience of trying to draw a three-year-old's blood, their ER visit amounted to only a shot in Clark's thigh and a take-home list of over-the-counter meds.

Cardic drove Claire's car home. Claire sat in the back, singing and soothing the tired baby.

"Go make some tea. I'll tuck him in."

"Just make sure he pees first."

Cardic took Clark to his room and changed him into clean pajamas.

"Hey, wake up, little man."

"Auntie, why you here? Where's Mommy?"

"That's my hello?"

Clark smiled and held up his little hand in greeting. Their secret handshake, as Clark called it, was more of just a wiggling of fingers. Cardic grabbed and held the soft hand in hers. She looked down and wondered what it would be like to come home to a sweet, sleepy child every night.

A redheaded child.

Whoa. Where'd that come from?

The anxiety and restlessness from the hospital returned, and Cardic made a hasty retreat home. She'd only be able to get a couple of good hours of sleep, and she was teaching three classes back-to-back tomorrow. Taking a cab would ensure she got at least four hours, but the skin-crawling feeling had her walking down Sheridan Street toward her apartment instead.

Why the thoughts about children? Her age maybe?

Cardic's mom seemed to be getting the picture that any more grandchildren would be Claire's burden to bear. And her father liked to remind her that the apple didn't fall far from the tree.

Spencer Lawson was a brilliant lawyer and a great dad when Cardic and her sister had been young children. But the happy childhood could mostly be accredited to her mother for putting up with so much bullshit. In high school, Cardic became aware of her father's many indiscretions.

At first, she thought it didn't bother her. But as she and her sister learned the truth, their mother lost interest in keeping up the ruse. She became depressed and lost interest in many things. The delicious homemade meals that Cardic had been spoiled by became more infrequent, and her father began spending even more late evenings at the office.

Around the same time, Cardic started to explore her sexuality, a lot. And she remembered one of the only things her dad said to her when she came out was that she too would be a lady-killer.

Lady-killer she was. Lying, cheating bastard she was not. Cardic never promised women anything, and she preferred the kind of woman who didn't expect promises. She wasn't about to get caught up in the drama, stress, and dissatisfaction that were the result of human beings attempting desperately to remain monogamous. Her attention span for one woman was limited, and she was honest about it.

❖

"Happy Friday!" Vivian bounced into the office and placed a large coffee on Olivia's desk.

"Thanks. Cream, no sugar?"

"Of course. I'd like to keep my job," Vivian joked as she

unpacked her laptop and sat at her desk just outside Olivia's office, leaving the door open.

Olivia shook her head at the bad joke and decided to pick up coffee for herself and Vivian next week. She'd never bought Vivian coffee. She didn't even know what she took in her coffee.

"Late night last night?"

Olivia looked up from the sales figures she'd been poring over since six thirty that morning. When she woke up at four after a restless sleep, she decided to come in early. "Why do you ask?" She tried not to sound defensive. Her date with Cardic hadn't lasted long at all, but the nagging arousal and back-and-forth arguments in her own mind had kept her up most of the night. She'd taken time getting ready before she left the house just after five thirty. Her makeup was flawless, and she'd put her hair up in a French twist. There was no way she looked like she hadn't slept.

"I know you're meeting with McKinnon Tuesday. I just thought you probably camped out here all night to prepare."

A week ago, that was probably exactly what Olivia would have done. But something about meeting Cardic, and their date last night, made her wish she had some scrap of a social life. Not that she'd admit that to anyone.

"Right. I'm sure I'll be prepared. He just wants updates on the marketing campaign and store contracts. All good news."

"Is this the final meeting before your brand overview is due? What do you need from me?"

Olivia looked up at Vivian, her back turned, typing away on her laptop, absentmindedly tapping her foot against the desk. She was a hard worker and always had a great attitude. Olivia realized at that moment how lost she'd be during this important time in her career if it weren't for Vivian.

"Just keep up the great work."

Olivia felt certain after a short lunch break she'd be able to concentrate and get all her notes finalized for her meeting with McKinnon. But staring at a blank document and the blinking cursor for five minutes was not very productive. She'd made her decision about a no-strings fling with Cardic, but doubts crept up every time thought of calling her.

Glancing at the White Sox tickets pinned to her large wall calendar, Olivia picked up the phone. She'd never in her life been indecisive, and she wasn't going to start now. Cardic turned her on. Cardic wanted her. And the chemistry was undeniable. A no-strings fling would help her concentrate at work and release some stress. They were both consenting adults. As soon as things got weird, Olivia would put an end to it.

When Cardic answered, Olivia glanced up to make sure Vivian was still away from her desk. "I'm sorry I had to leave so suddenly last night."

"No, I understand. I hope your nephew is all right." Olivia felt guilty for not asking right away, but her thoughts were on other things. Like the fact that she was about to agree to an affair with an almost stranger. After a couple minutes of small talk, Olivia took a deep breath. "No strings. No obligations. And I'm in control. Understood?"

"Oh yes. You free right now?"

Olivia giggled at the heat and humor in Cardic's sexy voice. "No, not right now." Olivia hesitated before mentioning the White Sox tickets. Was that too much like a date? No, not a date. This was a sexual arrangement. There would be no need for entertainment or conversation. Just sex. And good foreplay. This could be like extended foreplay. A buildup to the good stuff. Olivia felt better with a somewhat reasonable explanation for why they would ever need to be together outside the bedroom, so she continued. "I have tickets for the rivalry game tomorrow. Want to start with that?"

"As long as you end up naked on top of me, I don't care where we start."

Olivia was surprised at the blunt remark. They'd flirted and kissed, but Cardic had yet to say anything that raw and sexual to her. Picturing Cardic stripping out of her clothes and submitting to whatever Olivia asked of her would be a distracting image throughout the rest of her day.

❖

Cardic attempted to concentrate on what Davenport was saying, but all she could think about was sinking her fingertips into Olivia's moist flesh. She'd been in a painful state of arousal since Olivia called an hour ago and agreed to their "no-strings-attached" affair. She leaned back in her office chair as she gave Davenport a glare.

"So, due to the low enrollment, it's looking like we will only need you as adjunct next year."

Cardic locked gazes with Davenport. "Come again?"

"Next year. Adjunct. We won't need you full-time. Unless you can come up with a way to offer a master's level anthro class?"

"Is this because I tell the kids not to buy a fucking textbook?" Cardic's temper was close to the surface since so much of her energy was being utilized in not coming in her pants at thoughts of Olivia.

"I suggest watching your tone and language with me, Dr. Lawson."

Cardic exhaled slowly and gave Davenport a tight smile.

"I'm sorry, sir. I've got a class in a few minutes I need to prepare for. If you'll excuse me."

Cardic stalked into her office and threaded her hands through her hair, trying to get a grip. She knew Davenport didn't like her. She'd known that for a while. She didn't know or care why, and it hadn't affected her at all. Until now. She picked up the Intro to Anthropology book on her desk and threw it against the wall, knocking several photos of the Yanapo tribespeople to the floor.

"Hey, I just put those up!" Patrick screeched from behind Cardic, flying past her to pick up the notes and photos. "What the hell is your problem?"

After helping Patrick pick up the papers and photos, Cardic looked at the wall for the first time since that day Patrick had started putting everything in order. The pleasure and excitement she expected were lost, based on the news that she was basically out of a job next year. "I'm sorry, Pat. Just trying to let off some steam." Cardic didn't mention anything further to Patrick, not wanting to worry him. But why would he need to worry? There would surely be another professor in the department who could use a competent, motivated grad assistant.

Again, Cardic looked at the wall, the faces of her tribemates staring back at her. She searched out Yako's yellow eyes, as she often did when looking at photos of the people. He had a calming influence on her in the jungle; maybe the same would be true for Chicago.

The first picture she landed on was of Yako and a tribe woman named Nalya. She had recently given birth and was nursing her newborn as Yako looked on. The men were not very involved with child rearing, but Cardic had noticed Yako took more interest in the babies than some of the other men.

"Everything kosher, boss? It looks okay?"

After a moment of looking over the images of the people she had come to call family, a calm infused Cardic's body, and she felt ready to carry on with her day. "It looks great. I'll throw my book somewhere else next time." Cardic winked and grabbed her notes for her 102 class.

CHAPTER TEN

Cardic was a little disappointed at the mixture of shock and dread on Olivia's face when she opened her apartment door the next day. Olivia's hair was smooth, lacking its usual curl, and it was pulled away from her face with a black headband. Her red lips turned down in a frown, and Cardic was about to ask what was wrong when she noticed the sparkly White Sox logo spread across Olivia's tight T-shirt.

"Maybe this isn't going to work out," Olivia said as she backed away, attempting to hide her growing grin.

Cardic grabbed her 2016 World Series Championship baseball cap off the nearby hook and proudly slapped it down on her head backward. "It is a rivalry game, after all." Cardic's Chicago Cubs baseball T-shirt was old and worn, but she'd never get rid of it. It was a present from her dad before she found out what an asshole he really was and their relationship crumbled.

"I've never, ever slept with a Cubs fan."

After locking her front door, Cardic turned around and looked down at Olivia. In the small space of the two-flat foyer, she could smell Olivia's perfume. It was a sophisticated, dark smell, not like the flowery perfume a lot of the women she slept with wore.

Olivia's makeup was perfectly applied, and her lashes

were so long they almost touched her eyebrows when she blinked. Cardic took a step closer to Olivia and bent down to whisper in her ear. A whisper was all she intended, but Cardic found herself overwhelmed by the urge to trace the shell of Olivia's ear with her tongue.

"Would you like to sleep with a Cubs fan before or after the Cubbies win?"

"Confident, aren't you?" Olivia stepped back as Cardic trailed kisses down her neck. Her stomach tightened as Cardic reached a sensitive spot, and Olivia reached up to place her hands on Cardic's chest. She had every intention of pushing Cardic away, but Olivia nearly came out of her skin at the feel of Cardic's firm muscles under the worn cotton. How long had it been since she'd slept with someone? As hard as she tried, Olivia couldn't picture the last woman she'd slept with. Or remember when it happened. *Six months ago?* Olivia grabbed the nape of Cardic's neck and pulled her forward until their lips met.

Their bodies aligned and Cardic gently pushed Olivia against the wall, trailing her hand down Olivia's ribs and resting it on her hip. Olivia angled her head and pushed past Cardic's lips until their tongues met. The hand at her hip was firm but gentle, and Olivia found herself wishing that hand would mold to every inch of her body.

No, maybe eight months. It was that Brazilian girl from the conference in Dallas.

Not one to lose track of the moment, Olivia enjoyed the warm heat rushing through her but was soon feeling helpless to stop the onslaught of sensation. Her brain told her to shut it down, while her hands bunched the front of Cardic's T-shirt and tugged the strands of hair curling at the nape of Cardic's neck. As the tide continued to rush through her, Olivia pulled at every scrap of control and moved her mouth away from Cardic's talented kisses.

The look of desperation and just barely controlled restraint on Cardic's face was almost as intoxicating as the feel of her hard body and strong hands. Her eyes were heavy, and she licked her lips as she took off her ball cap and ran a hand through her hair, a mixture of frustration and pleasure on her handsome face, her jaw clenched.

If Olivia hadn't been determined to remain in control of their liaisons, it wouldn't have taken much convincing from that mouth to blow off the game and spend the afternoon in Cardic's bed. As it was, Olivia had every intention of scheduling, initiating, and dictating every detail of their affair.

Cardic still seemed to be playing by Olivia's rules as she relented, waved a hand toward the stairs, and said, "After you."

It was a fifteen-minute walk from Cardic's apartment to nearby Wrigleyville. The streets were lined with ash trees, and the leaves hadn't started changing colors yet since the weather had been so warm. As they neared the stadium, more people milled about, and it wasn't long before they were hustled into the stadium with hundreds of other fans.

"Wow, thank Joan for me. These seats are awesome," Cardic said as she stood by to let Olivia go first into the aisle of seats.

Heat emanated off Cardic's body, almost as if she suffered from a fever. Olivia could feel it as she brushed past her to sit down. Would she always be this acutely aware of Cardic's body? If so, maybe more outings like this were out of the question, and they should stick to sex.

"Unlike all you drunk Cubs fans, Joan actually gets tickets to watch the game. Not just binge drink to drown out the sorrows of pathetic losses."

Sitting down next to Olivia, Cardic placed her hand on her shirt and clutched her chest, "Ouch. Hit me where I live."

Olivia smirked as they both stood to sing the national anthem. The seats Joan picked were great. A lot of people liked being right behind home plate, but she and Joan had always preferred seats near first or third base. The field box was facing east, so the sun wasn't in their eyes, and they had a great view of home plate.

As the afternoon wore on, Cardic seemed to grow more comfortable with the tension between them, while it was only making Olivia more apprehensive. How could she survive an affair with someone when she jumped every time they brushed hands? As they climbed the stairs to Cardic's apartment, Olivia intended to tell her as much. *Maybe this was a bad idea.*

Unlocking her door and letting Olivia precede her inside, Cardic asked if Olivia wanted a drink and disappeared into the kitchen. Olivia glanced at the door and thought about making a run for it. She'd slept with plenty of women and had enjoyed some no-strings flings, but something about the chemistry with Cardic made her nervous that she was playing with fire. Playing with fire in a field of dry straw. One wrong move and everything in her well-ordered life would go up in flames.

"I know you're too turned on to leave." Cardic stood leaning against the doorway to the kitchen with two beer bottles dangling from her fingers. Her eyes moved up and down Olivia's body with such hunger that Olivia could feel it like a touch. Cardic looked relaxed, self-assured. And so sexy it hurt. Before Olivia could speak, Cardic licked her damn lips again. A quick dart of her tongue and Olivia was lost.

"You're in control, Olivia. What do you want?" Cardic's voice was husky and rough.

Olivia reminded herself of the agreement that she would be calling the shots. She changed gears and decided to concentrate on what came easily to her: control. She perused Cardic's body as Cardic had perused hers. She let her gaze drift from Cardic's broad shoulders, small breasts, and tight stomach to the slight flare of her hips that led to her strong thighs. Olivia's calm was replaced with an almost choking need to see Cardic's body.

"Take off your shirt," Olivia said as she backed up and sat on the worn sofa, ten feet away from Cardic.

The fact that Cardic set the beer bottles down and grabbed the hem of her T-shirt immediately with no argument didn't escape Olivia's attention. If Cardic was going to be this compliant, maybe this could work. As the bronze plane of Cardic's chest and stomach was revealed, Olivia held her breath. She was so distracted by the defined muscles of Cardic's chest, she almost didn't notice the softball-sized tattoo above her right breast. Olivia studied the tattoo. It resembled a Celtic knot but somehow seemed more natural with gentle curves and swirls. Vines and floral patterns braided together to form an intricate and symmetrical design. She was tempted to ask if Cardic had gotten the tattoo while in the jungle but thought perhaps that was too personal. They were only here to have sex, after all.

"Now unbutton your pants. But don't pull them down."

Olivia swallowed as Cardic's strong hands reached for her belt and zipper. The only sound in the room was Olivia's own breathing and the clinking of Cardic's belt.

For a moment, Olivia just stared. The veins in Cardic's arms were standing out as if straining her muscles was helping her remain in her state of subordination. Olivia could tell being told what to do did not come naturally to Cardic. Knowing this turned Olivia on even more.

When a few moments went by without Olivia giving another instruction, Cardic grabbed one of the discarded beers and popped the top. She took a long, cool sip and felt like she was about to explode, but she tried with all her might to hold it together. She wanted Olivia to know she was serious about letting her call the shots. All afternoon, Olivia went from flirty to distant and back again. Cardic felt sure she was having second thoughts about their agreement. But she could tell from the darkening green in Olivia's eyes that she wanted her. Cardic was walking a fine line between driving her crazy and driving her away.

Watching Olivia squirm on the couch was hard enough. Her tight blue jeans hugged her curves, and she kept rubbing her hands up and down her thighs, making Cardic's mouth water. Cardic needed some stimulation, or she was going to die here in her kitchen doorway.

Slowly, Cardic lifted her hand and rubbed her right nipple with her index and middle finger. The touch shot to her core like a lightning bolt.

Olivia's eyes widened, and she stopped squirming. "Come here."

Cardic took several steps to close the distance between them, aware that Olivia's eyes never left the fingers still rubbing her nipple.

When Cardic stopped just in front of her, Olivia took the beer bottle from Cardic's hand and took a sip. She grabbed Cardic's wrist and put it down at her side. "Stay."

Before she knew what Olivia was doing, the cool rim of the beer bottle replaced the warmth of her own fingers. She muttered a curse, and her hips jutted forward.

"Cold?" Olivia gave a wicked smile, and Cardic wondered how painful this game was going to be.

"It's fine," Cardic gasped. Cardic had experimented with all kinds of toys and games, and she'd never been able to raise the bar on her arousal. The bar was pretty high to begin with. But one look from Olivia, one command, and one cold beer bottle later, she felt like a teenager about to go off in the backseat of a car.

Olivia darted her eyes to the hallway. "Bedroom back there?"

Cardic nodded her head, not trusting herself to speak.

Olivia put the beer bottle on the coffee table and grabbed Cardic's hand. Cardic watched the sway of Olivia's hips as she walked toward the bedroom.

Cardic's bedroom was sparsely furnished. The room was really only used for sleeping and occasionally watching movies on the wall-mounted flat screen TV. There were no pictures or knickknacks. As she noticed Olivia glance around, she wondered if it seemed stale or boring. In that moment, she also realized she'd never had sex with a woman in this room.

Her thoughts were derailed when Olivia pulled her T-shirt up over her head, revealing a dark green lace bra. It matched her eyes.

"I have every intention of staying for a while, but I won't be sleeping here."

Olivia pulled at the zipper of her jeans and shimmied out of them.

Matching panties.

They hadn't really discussed the rules at all. Cardic's fingers itched to rip those flimsy panties away from Olivia's porcelain skin, but she didn't know if the act would be welcomed. Was she just supposed to stand here and be commanded? What if she wanted something else? What if she *needed* something else?

In an almost shy voice, Olivia said, "Kiss me." Half command, half plea.

To someone else, it might have seemed almost as if Olivia was a sweet, innocent girl about to engage in lovemaking for the first time. The small, unsure sound was so uncharacteristic of Olivia that Cardic felt a pull at something inside her. Or maybe it was just the Wrigley Field chili dog. Cardic decided to ignore the unwelcome twinge of emotion and concentrated on the rise and fall of Olivia's ample chest as she moved closer.

Olivia seemed hungry for contact as her hands came to rest on Cardic's shoulders and squeezed. Cardic used less finesse than she intended as she slid her tongue into Olivia's mouth, but something about the dynamic made her feel less inhibited with her own response. Olivia was calling the shots, and Cardic felt free to act in a way she never had before. To act as if her control wasn't in question and she didn't need to hold it together for anything. It was liberating. And hot.

Their mouths separated as they caught their breath and Olivia slid her hands down Cardic's stomach to pull at her open jeans. Rather than balling her fists at her sides, her initial instinct in this situation, Cardic palmed one of Olivia's breasts. Olivia threw her head back and moaned as Cardic used her other hand to rid herself of her pants and boxers. Olivia removed her bra and panties as she pushed herself farther toward Cardic's touch.

They tumbled naked onto the bed, and Cardic moved her hands in a rush over Olivia's body. She wanted to explore every dip and curve. She felt desperate to touch as much of Olivia as she could at once.

Fighting the familiar urge to climb on top of Olivia and take control, Cardic relaxed back into the pillows as Olivia threw her leg over Cardic's body to anchor her onto the bed.

"I'm going to make you come now. But you have to lie still." Olivia's eyes smoldered at Cardic as she moved down her body.

When Olivia's warm lips closed around her nipple, Cardic

bucked her hips, frantic for more contact. More pressure. More anything.

Olivia removed her mouth and glared at Cardic. "I said lie still."

Before complying, Cardic reached up to remove the elastic band holding up Olivia's hair. As those fiery waves spilled across her chest like lava, Cardic placed her hands on the bed, determined to follow Olivia's commands so she'd end this torture.

Cardic clenched her teeth together and held her breath as Olivia bathed her chest and stomach with her hot mouth, adding gentle nips and tugs of her teeth when she found a sensitive spot. As Olivia neared the apex of her thighs, Cardic knew it'd take nothing more than a swipe of that tongue to send her over. The desperation and near pain canceled out any embarrassment she might have felt at losing it so quickly.

Olivia ran her hands up and down Cardic's thighs in one last teasing move before finally settling her mouth over Cardic's moist heat. Cardic ignored Olivia's breathy command to lie still and leaned up on one elbow to grab a fistful of Olivia's hair as she feasted on Cardic's sensitive flesh. Cardic contracted her abs and arched her back, trying to make it last. But when she felt a moan escape Olivia's lips, it reverberated through her every atom, and she came apart with a shout.

Olivia wouldn't relent and kept her mouth against the pulse of Cardic's center, pulling every last wave of sensation from her weakened body. Cardic collapsed back on the pillows and let out a shaky breath.

"Holy shit."

... she started to cry, and she used her hand to swipe a tear, and when she felt a tear escape, threw a hasty arm across her ... through her own mouth and swallowed it with a hard ... Olivia would ... clean and kept her mouth against the palm of Chole's temer, trailing over a last wave of emotion from her weakened body ... she slumped back on the pillows and let out a shaky breath.

"Holy shit."

CHAPTER ELEVEN

You can say that again.
Olivia was no stranger to making women come, but that was the most magical thing she'd ever experienced. She watched her own hands as she rubbed Cardic's still sensitive flesh, then glanced up at Cardic.

Her arms were thrown out to her sides, her eyes still closed, her breath coming in sharp, short gasps. Cardic's muscles were relaxed but still defined, and she had a slight sheen of sweat on her face and neck. Having complete power and control of this strong, sexual creature was an intense high.

Amazing.

It was common for Olivia to make her lover come twice before she would attempt to reach orgasm herself, but Cardic's response to her touch had been so electrifying, she was coming apart and couldn't wait any longer. This was her show and Olivia didn't feel ashamed of wanting to get off. Olivia felt pleased and almost shy when Cardic opened her coffee eyes and began touching and rubbing her stomach and breasts.

"Your body is amazing. I can't stop touching you."

Olivia ignored the comment and continued her trek up Cardic's body until her thighs rested on either side of Cardic's head.

"You're going to make me come now. Fast."

Olivia had meant her tone to be light and playful, but the heat and hunger in Cardic's eyes almost made her come without contact.

Cardic grabbed Olivia's hips and pulled her down hard onto her mouth, her eyes never leaving Olivia's face. Her mouth was wet and so hot it almost burned. Olivia cried out and grabbed the upholstered headboard to brace herself. She couldn't remember the last time she had been this turned on, and with the divine tongue beneath her, she realized she couldn't remember the last time she'd come so fast.

Breaking eye contact only increased the tenacity of Cardic's actions as she palmed Olivia's ass and sucked at her flesh.

"Yes, oh my God." Olivia bit her lip and tried not to scream as she ground her hips into Cardic's face, not caring how wanton or desperate she seemed. As warm waves of pleasure slid through her, Olivia kept her hold on the headboard, trying not to lose her balance.

Intending to move away from Cardic to gain back her footing, Olivia was surprised when Cardic flipped her over and climbed on top of her.

"Again, please," Cardic begged in a rough voice as she straddled Olivia's thigh, elbows locked and looking down at Olivia with desperation.

"Yes, yes, Cardic." Olivia grabbed Cardic's ass and encouraged her frantic movements.

As Cardic pumped her hips and breathed hard in her ear, Olivia was amazed to feel herself on the brink again. Pulling Cardic hard against her, Olivia matched Cardic's thrusts and came again in a rush of heat.

"Where have you been all my life?" Cardic said as she regained control of her breathing.

"Glad it wasn't too difficult for you to surrender control. I had my doubts."

"Hey, whatever gets you there. I'm easy to please."

"Apparently."

Cardic looked over at Olivia's body covered by the light sheet. She didn't remember when or how they ended up under the covers. Olivia's luscious curves were outlined in the stark white, and Cardic reached over to caress her hip. Even after the most intense orgasm of her life, shock waves still shot through her when she touched Olivia's skin.

"Do you usually bottom so easily?" Olivia grinned. Her lipstick had rubbed off, giving the lower half of her face a pink glow, but the rest of her makeup was flawless as usual. Her hair even fell in perfect curls around her shoulders.

"If the situation calls for it, which it rarely does. But after I had your mouth on me, it was rather easy to let go."

Cardic's dark eyes seemed to get even darker, and her hands grew more insistent. Olivia didn't know how she expected this encounter to go, but she thought Cardic would have a little more trouble surrendering to her. The lack of opposition was unexpected, and more of a turn-on than Olivia thought it would be. Or wanted it to be.

Before her thoughts could contaminate the lazy aftermath of the experience, Olivia jumped up to get dressed. Cardic grabbed at her playfully as she scooted away.

"You're leaving already? I thought we could go for round two."

"Didn't you already get to round two?" Olivia laughed at the look on Cardic's face, like she'd been busted making out in the high school bathroom.

Cardic flopped back on the bed, the sheet now at her waist, unconcerned and unashamed of her nakedness. She laced her fingers behind her head, watching Olivia get dressed. "When can I see you again?"

"I'm busy at work, but I'm sure I'll have some free time next week." Olivia brushed aside the disappointment she felt at Cardic being okay going a week without having sex with her again. Olivia was already cataloging ways to tease Cardic and the unusual positions she wanted to try.

A nude Cardic walked Olivia to the door and stopped with her hand on the doorknob. "Do I say thank you?"

"It's really not necessary—" Before she could finish her thought, that wicked tongue made its way into her mouth and Olivia tried to keep herself from moaning. "See you next week. I'll call you."

Sometime later, Cardic was woken from a restful sleep by the phone ringing. Cardic stretched and smiled at the soreness and pleased state of her body, then reached over to grab the phone. The caller ID read Claire, and Cardic was almost embarrassed to pick it up. It seemed weird to talk to her sister this soon after having sex. She reluctantly answered, knowing Claire would worry if she went too long without answering.

After exchanging pleasantries and talking to Clark for a minute, Cardic attempted small talk. "So what's up with you? Plans for the party coming along okay?"

"Yeah, fine. You sound great. I thought you'd be pissed since your conversation with Davenport."

A cold breeze blew through Cardic as she recalled the fact that she might not be employed next fall. The anticipation of seeing Olivia and the surreal experience of taking her to bed had pushed everything else from Cardic's mind. So much for postcoital bliss. As Cardic sat up and glanced at the clock, she pulled on her boxers.

"Davenport is an asshole. You know I'll figure everything out. I don't want you to worry."

"Listen to you. Your job is in jeopardy, and you're worried about me," Claire said.

Cardic knew Claire didn't need her to worry, but she did just the same. Even when they were kids, she'd been that way. Claire was such an important person in her life, she valued her and Clark's well-being above her own.

"I've got some data to look through. Call me tomorrow, and let me know how soccer practice goes." Cardic tried not to laugh because watching Clark play soccer was like watching a puppy learn how to ice-skate. He must have gotten his poor coordination from his deadbeat dad.

"Okay, and don't forget, I need you at the party early to help set up."

Cardic felt guilty for hoping the day of Clark's party wouldn't be the only day Olivia would be available to get together again next week. Time spent with her nephew should always outweigh sex. No matter how mind-blowing, satisfying, or dream inspiring. "I'll be there."

As she walked into the dining room with Cicero trailing behind her, she glanced at the dozens of boxes of data and notes she needed to catalog and analyze. The task seemed daunting, but at least it would keep her from replaying her night with Olivia over and over.

❖

"It's Joan on line two. She's insistent this time."

Olivia looked up from the planogram she was studying and cringed at the phone. Truthfully, she'd had several breaks between meetings today where she could have returned Joan's nine thousand phone calls, but she'd been avoiding it. Joan knew her better than anyone on earth, even her dad. And as soon as Olivia spoke, Joan would know she'd been with

Cardic. Wanting to avoid the third degree, Olivia cleared her throat and practiced her authoritarian voice before picking up.

"Hey, Joan. Sorry, I've been swamped today."

"Yeah, what else is new. I'll be in the area and wanted to catch you for lunch. My boss made reservations at Butcher's Block to meet with a client, but they canceled. He said I could have them. Meet you there at twelve thirty?"

Olivia's mouth watered. They'd both been talking about the new steakhouse for months since it opened but figured they'd have to wait for the craze to die down. It had already been named in local papers and magazines as the new restaurant to try. Olivia hesitated. "Umm...pass?" Olivia cringed, waiting for Joan's reaction, then pressed save on the deck she was working on and closed all her files. She could already taste a juicy rib eye. And there was no way Joan would let her pass this up.

"Ha, yeah, right. See you soon." Joan hung up, not waiting for an argument or reply.

Butcher's Block was not far from Olivia's office, and the brisk walk to the restaurant helped her burn off some energy. Sleep had eluded her lately, and she'd been tortured by thoughts of Cardic's talented mouth and hard body, which wasn't unpleasant but hadn't made for a very productive morning.

As she entered the restaurant, she was greeted by a friendly and attractive hostess who led her to a table near the bank of windows in the back, facing the river. The ceilings were high with exposed beams and ductwork running in every direction. Each of the high-top tables appeared to be an actual butcher's block or at least fashioned to look like it. Olivia smoothed her hand over the slightly grooved, wood-grained surface and thanked the server for the glass of water he set before her. As she sat in the posh steakhouse trying to focus on the extensive menu of steaks, ribs, and seafood, all Olivia could see were the cords of Cardic's muscles flexing as she came apart below her. *Delicious.*

"Does the menu look that good? You're drooling." Joan dropped her briefcase and sat down with a plop, bringing Olivia back to the present.

"I'm sure everything is delicious. I'm assuming you've already looked at the menu online. Any suggestions?"

"I know it's a steakhouse, but I'm leaning toward the bourbon glazed salmon with garlic and leek mashed potatoes." Joan pulled off her stylish sunglasses and pushed her menu aside. "I saw we kicked the ass outta those Cubs. Did you and your dad enjoy the game?"

Olivia glanced around, hoping the server would return and save her from what was about to be a total blunder. "Did we enjoy the game? Yeah. I mean, yes. It was great."

Joan quirked a perfect blond eyebrow. "So are you lying about enjoying the game or who you went with?"

Being busted lying by Joan was nothing new. Neither was her dragging out Olivia's embarrassment at her inability to lie to her convincingly. "I'm not lying."

"You always lie about lying when you're lying. You also repeat questions I just asked you. Spill. Were you with the good doctor, by chance?"

"You act like she's a brain surgeon."

Joan pumped her fist and laughed out loud. "Ha! I knew it. Was it just the game or...more?" Her endless dark lashes started batting. Thankfully, the server arrived then to take their order, giving Olivia some time to formulate her thoughts and dry her sweaty palms. She couldn't help the beating pulse that raced to her core when she again thought of Cardic's hot, naked body and her desperation to climax.

"We spent some time together."

Not enough time.

"How did it go?" Joan asked.

"It was fine."

Steamy. Erotic. Astounding.

The look on her face told Olivia Joan knew pressing for more details now would lead nowhere. After all, Joan thought of Olivia as some sort of passive-aggressive volcano. When things became too great, overwhelming, or intense, she'd blow. It did seem odd, even to Olivia, that she wouldn't share intimate details of fantastic sex with her best friend. It was not uncommon for Olivia to kiss and tell.

"Are you going to see her again?"

Olivia paused before answering as the server dropped off their drinks, knowing she needed to explain the situation to Joan before she got the wrong idea. She and Cardic were going to be sleeping together, not beginning a relationship. "We have come to an agreement."

Joan looked intrigued. "What kind of agreement?"

"Well, we sort of…I mean I guess we've…"

Joan looked at Olivia with a face that said she was trying to be patient. "You've…?"

Olivia hated stumbling over her words. It never happened in her professional life, and in her personal life it usually only happened with Joan. Olivia straightened her spine and blurted, "We've decided to continue sleeping together."

After Joan's lack of response, Olivia tasted her own cocktail. Olivia didn't normally drink on her lunch break, but something about her relationship, no, the *arrangement* with Cardic and now spilling the beans to Joan required some liquid courage.

"Olive. Why the cagey attitude? You've had affairs before. And shared the juicy details. I'll expect the same courtesy this time." Joan winked as the server brought two amazing-looking Caesar salads with homemade croutons. "I think it's great you'll be letting loose a little."

"Right. Maybe the outlet for energy will even help me at work."

"It's not all about work, Olive."

Of course it was. Work was safe. Work was predictable. At work, Olivia was in control.

I'm in control with Cardic. That's part of the arrangement.

Somehow Olivia felt like that was the furthest thing from the truth.

CHAPTER TWELVE

Cardic leaned back in her chair, lacing her fingers behind her head to admire the scattered notes, pictures, and diagrams now covering the back wall of her office. Patrick complained about the "mess," saying everything would be easier to access in the program on her laptop, but Cardic felt at ease staring at the last eighteen months of her life labeled and categorized in a way she could understand and easily view.

A photo of the bright red *camu camu* fruit caught her eye. It was typical practice for a man interested in sleeping with a woman to bring her a piece of the purple cherry-like fruit to express his interest in mating with her. Cardic loved this tradition because it didn't seem silly and romantic like bringing flowers to a first date. Somehow, to her at least, it seemed to send a more direct message. Also more practical, as the fruit was delicious.

A knock on her office door brought her back to the present. "It's open."

"Hey, Doc. Your dad is on line two."

Cardic rolled her eyes and waved Patrick out of the office as she grabbed the phone, hoping this would be quick.

"What's up, Pop?"

"Cardic, where have you been all week? It's impossible to get in touch with you."

Cardic could hear the smile in her father's voice. No doubt he thought she worked all day, then partied all night with an array of beautiful women. For some reason, the thought that she was a sex-crazed womanizer seemed to give him a sense of pride. Cardic didn't have the inclination or desire to correct him. "The semester is really heating up. And I've got to get through more of this data before the holidays."

"The holidays. That's actually why I'm calling. I can't make our golf trip in November. Shelly wants to head to Bali for Thanksgiving."

Shelly, the current trophy. She'd been hanging on to Cardic's father the past three or four years. He liked to have a "girlfriend" to keep up appearances at work and charity functions. Shelly spent his money, and he slept with anyone he wanted to. A match made in heaven.

"Bali. I hear it's beautiful this time of year." The sarcasm was lost on Spencer. Cardic had inherited that trait from her mother.

The strained conversation ended not a moment too soon, and Cardic packed up to leave. The anticipation of seeing Olivia tonight made the hours crawl by. She felt rushed and antsy and even dismissed her last class ten minutes early, which was not common practice for her. It had been over a week since they'd slept together, and Cardic was crawling out of her skin. She was distracted at work, and all she could do at night was relive their all-too-brief encounter.

In the jungle, Cardic would wake up before dawn and pray for the sun. She loved nighttime in the jungle, but the predawn hours made her feel restless and uneasy, as if there was something worthwhile to do, but she had to wait for the lazy sunshine to appear. The Yanapo didn't stir until after dawn. Sometimes the village stayed quiet until eight or eight thirty. Cardic considered this "sleeping late," and even on her last morning in the Amazon, she'd had to wait for her tribemates to wake up before she could begin her last day with them.

But all the endless hours spent waiting for daylight in the jungle didn't hold a candle to the nagging feeling of time almost going backward in anticipation of seeing Olivia. Olivia had invited her over to her place, and Cardic was determined to get more time in bed with her. She didn't intend to leave until Olivia kicked her out the door. Cardic stopped to run her hands through her hair, wondering how long it had been since she'd been distracted by thoughts of a woman. College? High school maybe?

"I'm heading out." Patrick peered around the door and waved a paper at Cardic. "Some lady called while you were on the phone with your dad. I got her name and number. See you Monday." He was out the door before Cardic could respond. Patrick lived for nightlife, and he hated when Cardic asked him to stay at work late on Fridays.

After one last look around the office to make sure she had everything she needed, Cardic grabbed the message from Patrick and stuffed it in her pocket. She debated calling Olivia to mention she was on her way but feared Olivia would change her mind about getting together. The tangible chemistry between them was intense, and Cardic hadn't examined too closely what that meant. Even when they spoke on the phone, Cardic could hear the anxiety in Olivia's voice. Cardic didn't need or want to chase unwilling women. If she hadn't also heard the arousal, she probably would have put an end to this already. That and the fact that she'd received several sexually explicit text messages from Olivia during the week.

Cardic felt rushed and turned on already as she weaved her way down the crowded Friday-night streets of Olivia's neighborhood. After getting off the train, she stopped at a small farmer's market and bought a little white pumpkin for

Olivia, in honor of the tradition of the Yanapo. She intended to have mind-blowing sex all night with Olivia, so she felt it was the least she could do.

When Olivia opened the door to her a few minutes later, all the breath left her lungs. Cardic let her gaze wander down Olivia's body before she even entered her apartment. Her fiery red hair was falling loose and curly around her shoulders. She wore a simple black polo and tight jeans. Cardic never considered herself a foot person one way or the other. She looked down at Olivia's feet, with dark red polish on her little toenails, and all she wanted to do was drop to her knees and kiss those cute toes.

"Come in," Olivia said as she opened the door wider. Cardic could tell she was wondering about the pumpkin as she eyed the tiny fruit.

Cardic suddenly felt self-conscious about the silly gesture but knew it was too late now. Cardic stepped into Olivia's apartment and handed her the small pumpkin, attempting to seem causal about it. "When a Yanapo man wants to sleep with a woman, he brings her a small fruit to express his interest in sex with her."

Olivia smiled, turning the pumpkin over in her hands. A real smile that touched her eyes and transformed her face. She was breathtaking.

Seeming to catch herself in such a genuine smile, she straightened her full lips and glanced toward the kitchen. Her apartment was much more spacious than Cardic's, and a lot neater. There weren't papers scattered about, there was no mail on the entry table. The only thing that looked slightly askew was a pair of black pumps resting by the door and a knitted gray blanket thrown over the back of the large white sofa. On second glance, Cardic realized Olivia had probably painstakingly arranged the blanket to look that way.

The apartment was a corner unit, so there were huge windows near two of the living room walls. Olivia had opened the windows to a light breeze, so the sheer curtains were flowing slightly. There were several small lamps turned on in the room, but the light was soft. The setting struck Cardic as somewhat romantic. She felt a moment of panic.

But why? They both agreed to this arrangement. Unlike some other women Cardic had been with, Olivia had not only agreed to their no-strings affair, but she seemed more intent to sticking to the rules than Cardic.

She followed Olivia through the living room, noticing all the art on the walls. Framed pictures of vintage magazine covers and abstract art. No family pictures anywhere.

"I hope you like pork chops. I'm not much of a cook, but it's my dad's recipe. Are you hungry?"

Cardic watched Olivia's swaying hips and rounded ass as she walked toward the kitchen. Cardic caught up to her and placed her hands on Olivia's hips to turn her around. As their eyes met, Olivia licked her lips and leaned back against the large kitchen island.

Cardic tried to control the rising tide within her, remembering the rules, remembering that she wasn't in charge. If she was in charge, they'd already be naked. Cardic ran her hand to the nape of Olivia's neck and moved her mouth closer, still squeezing at her hip. Olivia's eyes held no question or hesitance as Cardic lowered her mouth to Olivia's dark red lips.

She tasted like wine and heat and something dark and dangerous. Olivia grabbed at Cardic's shirt and opened her legs wider, allowing Cardic to rub her thigh against her crotch. Olivia felt strong but pliant, and Cardic wanted to devour her.

As Olivia rubbed against her thigh more insistently, Cardic felt torn. Every fiber of her being told her to throw this gorgeous creature over her shoulder and take her to bed. But as badly as she wanted to feel those thick thighs wrapped around her, she wanted more to stay at a pace she knew Olivia would tolerate. Or they'd never make it to the bedroom.

"Tell me what you want," Cardic said, breathing into Olivia's open mouth. God, everything this woman did was sexy. Olivia stood there pulling at Cardic with her mouth wide open, breathing heavy. Her eyes locked on Cardic's mouth.

"Put your hand in my jeans."

"Yes." Cardic tore at Olivia's jeans and took a brief moment to admire the smooth, porcelain flesh of her belly between her opened fly and the hem of her shirt.

"Quick. The oven timer says we only have three minutes until dinner's ready," Olivia said, and Cardic was surprised at the note of humor in her voice.

"We won't need that long."

Olivia stared at Cardic's devilish grin and returned her own small smile until she felt Cardic's warm fingers touch the skin just above her panties. Her mind went blank, and she bit her lip to keep from making an embarrassing sound. Olivia squirmed, hoping Cardic would move her hand lower, inside, anywhere. Everywhere.

"Inside your panties? Or just in your jeans?"

"Fucking tease." Olivia grabbed Cardic's face with both hands and kissed her with everything she had. Nipping at her tongue, sucking at her lips. When Cardic finally moaned and tightened her hold, Olivia knew she'd made her point. "Just make me come."

Without hesitation, Cardic entered her and began a slow roll with the heel of her hand, hitting Olivia's clit in just the right spot.

"Oh, yes. So good."

Cardic leaned her head against Olivia's shoulder as she

worked magic with her hands. "Let's skip dinner. I can just stay inside you all night. I'm not hungry for food," Cardic whispered.

Those heated words and the onslaught of sensation pushed Olivia over the edge. She leaned back against the counter and let out a low moan and felt herself falling back to earth. The oven timer beeping pulled Olivia from her relaxed state. Why did she even ask Cardic over for dinner? She should have just asked her over for sex. How was she going to get through a meal when all she wanted to do was rip Cardic's clothes off?

"I've been thinking about that all week." Cardic ran a hand through her hair as she pulled her other hand from Olivia's pants.

Olivia stood up straight and zipped and buttoned her jeans. "What? Fucking me in my kitchen?" Olivia had had many sexual encounters in her own home, but nothing in recent memory had been this erotic. Or satisfying.

Cardic placed her hand on her chest and rubbed the muscle that lay under her tattoo. It was a habit Olivia had noticed, but she hadn't figured out yet what it meant.

"Kitchen. Bedroom. Tub. Wherever."

Olivia grabbed another wine glass from the cabinet, filled it, and handed it to Cardic. With a sickeningly sweet tone, she asked, "How was your day, dear?"

Cardic laughed out loud. Olivia had to admit, she'd never made dinner for anyone she was sleeping with. It was a paradox because this was all about sex, but at this moment, the entire thing seemed sort of…domestic.

"Work is good. I've got a really bright class this year for one of my beginning anthropology classes. My grad assistant and I are almost done organizing and cataloging the data from my time with the Yanapo. Then the real fun begins."

"What does that entail?"

"I'll be going through everything with a fine-tooth comb. Looking for patterns, examining customs and traditions." Cardic paused to gauge Olivia's expression. Many people zoned out when she started talking about work, especially her time in the Amazon. People wanted to know about the bugs, the animals, the weapons. Not many people she spoke to were interested in what had really touched Cardic about the experience.

Olivia seemed content to listen, and she asked insightful questions, so Cardic felt certain she was paying attention, even if she weren't truly interested. But something told Cardic she was. She continued. "It's funny, when I left for my field study I was scared I wouldn't be able to take enough notes. Like if I wanted to remember anything, I'd have to write it down. But I can remember everything so clearly...sometimes I wake up at night and believe I'm still there."

Olivia was caught off guard by Cardic's admission. Not just her words but the delivery. She had such a connection to the tribe she lived with for so long. And she wasn't ashamed or embarrassed to show that emotion or caring.

Cardic felt as though Olivia was examining her in some way, so she cleared her throat and changed the subject. "You didn't have to cook," she said, indicating the covered dishes on the stove. "I'm sure you're busy with work."

An image of Melissa's tight face and squawky voice invaded Olivia's brain as she served plates high with mashed potatoes, pork chops, and green beans. Her most recent interactions with Melissa might be the reason Olivia was so eager to see Cardic. She knew orgasmic relief would help her forget about work, or at least push it to the back of her mind.

"I guess...when you work as hard as I do, you expect everyone to see your vision. And when they don't, it's..."

"Frustrating?"

"Infuriating."

"What aren't they getting? I know the branding work you did for Vital's line of women's golf shirts." Cardic paused for emphasis and held up three fingers. "Third bestselling in the country, am I right?"

"Yes."

"That's what I thought. I own several myself. I'm sure that level of expertise and impressive work history count for something?"

"I'd be delighted if that were the case. But there's still some resistance to mainstream plus-size clothing."

"Why?"

"I'm really not sure. Being plus-size myself, it just makes sense that I should be able to walk into any store and buy what I want. But there's a negative connotation to being plus-size. A plus-size woman must be lazy. She must be unhealthy. She doesn't take pride in her appearance."

"Bullshit. Didn't you almost knock me out while jogging the day we met? I'm assuming that wasn't the first time you've jogged by the lake. Or the last."

Olivia was pleased and surprised by the slight note of defensiveness in Cardic's tone. "Many plus-size women are used to the stereotypes. What I want Vital's new plus-size line to convey is that no matter what your size, we have what you need. We're inclusive, affordable, quality fitness wear."

When Olivia looked up from her plate, Cardic was grinning. "What?" Olivia took a sip of her wine and waited, feeling a little foolish about climbing on her soapbox.

"Are you this passionate about everything?"

"What do you mean?"

"Well, I know you're passionate about sex. About being

in charge. Now I see how passionate you are at work. Don't you get tired of putting one hundred and ten percent into everything?" Cardic shook her head and continued eating.

"Oh, like you don't? Didn't you mention graduating from high school a year early? And there aren't many people who could leave their home and family for a year and a half that aren't completely invested into their career. So, is that level of passion exhausting to you?"

"Touché." Cardic pointed her fork at Olivia as she finished chewing. "And more avoidance. I'm going to crack you one of these days, Olivia. And it's going to be sweet."

Olivia asked if Cardic was finished and cleared their plates. Crack her? If Olivia wasn't careful, she was going to be shattered into a million pieces.

Chapter Thirteen

Olivia flopped forward onto the mattress after her third orgasm. "I can't help coming when you do that. I wasn't even trying that time."

That was when Cardic went down on her from behind. While Olivia was used to giving that kind of attention, she found it rather exhilarating to be on the receiving end. The feel of Cardic's body behind her, the anonymity of not seeing Cardic's face. And being able to somewhat hide her own reactions. Except for the noises. *God, I hope Mrs. Harper doesn't complain to the HOA.*

Cardic crawled up behind Olivia and spooned her, caressing her breasts. Olivia assumed Cardic did this to sexualize the intimate act of spooning. They both had their own subtle ways of reminding each other what kind of an arrangement they had agreed to. *Sex. It's just sex.*

"Well, I could just spend the night and wake you up that way in the morning. Just picture it. Coming before you've even had your coffee." Cardic nuzzled Olivia's neck and bit the tender flesh there.

"Sorry, no sleepovers."

Cardic grabbed for Olivia as she moved to get out of bed. "Come on. It's nearly four. It's almost morning anyway."

Since she and Cardic had been spending time together, Olivia thought she could pick up Cardic's humor pretty easily, so she wasn't overly concerned about the current conversation. One that was testing her limits. "Then you'd better get dressed and go." Olivia bent over to pick up Cardic's pants and hand them to her as she crawled out of bed with a little kid frown. Olivia tried to suppress a giggle.

"You're laughing? You know what's funny?" Cardic pulled Olivia's naked body against hers and held her tight, palming her ass and kissing her neck. "When you wake up tomorrow and want my mouth on you, my fingers inside you, you'll only have yourself to thank."

Olivia shuddered, her arousal returned with a vengeance. "Point taken."

Cardic winked and bent to put on her pants. A crumpled paper fell from her pocket, and Olivia picked it up. She had no intention of reading it, but a woman's name caught her eye. At first, she didn't know or care if it was business or pleasure, but the more she thought about it, the stranger she felt. "You dropped this."

Olivia watched Cardic's face for any sign of what this person meant to her.

"Oh, yeah a message from earlier. An old colleague." Cardic gave a tight smile and continued getting dressed.

As Olivia watched inch after inch of that beautiful body disappear under layers of clothes, she realized the alarming fact that she didn't want Cardic to leave. Even though they were done with sex, Olivia still wasn't ready for her to go. All the more reason to get rid of her.

Olivia grabbed her black silk robe and wandered out into the living room while Cardic finished dressing. She walked out in her pressed khakis, only a little wrinkled from being on the floor all night; her light blue button-down; and brown loafers. Her hair was disheveled but still somehow perfect. So handsome.

Cardic stared at Olivia as she pulled her watch from her pocket and clasped it around her wrist. "So, I'll call you later in the week? Will you have some time?"

"Sure, sure. Yeah."

Cardic nodded, kissed Olivia on the mouth, and headed for the door.

As she made her way down the early morning street, Cardic turned around to stare at Olivia's windows for a moment. Cardic hadn't wanted to leave. She couldn't remember a time when she'd spent an evening with a woman and hadn't been itching to get away. Unsettling. Of course, she'd never had sex this good either.

Megan would be a distant second. Very distant.

Megan. What did she want?

Cardic hadn't spoken to Megan in nearly ten years. Since their very messy breakup. Their failed relationship only further cemented in Cardic's mind that she was not cut out for domesticity, and though she'd been faithful through their relationship, her head turned easily, and she often felt trapped by Megan's jealous attitude. They'd had chemistry in the bedroom, but that's where the compatibility ended. Megan had always wanted Cardic to take charge, set the pace, make the decisions.

Being bossed around in the bedroom was different than Cardic had expected. She thought she would feel submissive and subordinate. But she didn't. She felt empowered by taking orders from Olivia about where to touch her, when to go slow, when to go fast. And many times, after things got going, she could anticipate Olivia's needs, and no words were even spoken.

Seeing Olivia's pale skin against the dark silk of that

robe, her hard nipples outlined to perfection, sent a shot straight to Cardic's clit. She'd wanted to linger and set a firm date for when they'd see each other next, but Olivia was too tempting in the dark, wrapped in silk, her hair hanging over her shoulders.

Cardic had pined for Olivia for weeks before they actually slept together. The relief of that was short-lived. Only days after, she was tortured by thoughts of Olivia's naked body and perfect breasts. Now, after their second encounter, Cardic felt as if there was no relief in sight. All she wanted to do was turn around, pound on her door, and beg Olivia to let her come back in.

"What the fuck is wrong with me?"

❖

The fall in Chicago was one of Olivia's favorite things. The crisp air, everyone bundled up in their warm scarves and hats. Fewer pigeons. The wonderful season almost made it easy to wait for her dad at their monthly meeting place. Almost, but not quite. She loved having a standing date with her father but hated what it tended to do to her schedule. Their meeting spot was never crowded and had a great view of the river. The hostess led Olivia straight to their usual table on the back patio, overlooking the river walk. Olivia was thankful for the shade of the small white oak tree. The weather was starting to get cooler, but she'd had enough of the summer sun.

All week she was kicking herself for spending Friday evening with Cardic. Those precious hours of the evening were like a dead zone at the Vital office, and she could have gotten tons of work done. As it was, she worked Monday through Friday from six a.m. to eight p.m., while the office was teeming with people, and her phone never stopped ringing and her unread messages multiplying by the minute. She often felt like she was chipping away at her to-do list with a toothpick.

After that thought left her head, it was replaced by the guilt of bitching when she was so lucky to have her dad in her life. She knew lots of friends from college whose parents wouldn't speak to them once they came out. Her dad had always been there for her. Her coming out was a non-issue. She figured he attributed her being a lesbian to the fact that her mother left. *As if being gay was the result of some trauma.* She knew many people of his generation felt that way. But Olivia still remembered little Ashley back in kindergarten. She used to chase Ashley around the playground and always wanted to put her hair in pigtails. Any reason to be close to her.

When Olivia noticed her dad approach, she pushed all thoughts aside and forced a smile. He could always read her pretty well, and she didn't want him to worry, "Hey. Daddy."

"Hey, Olive Bug. You look beautiful. Something new going on at work?"

"No, same old same old. We're almost ready for the line to go out. A lot going on. The usual stress."

"Stress? You look more relaxed than I've seen in years. I thought maybe you'd met someone."

Olivia nearly laughed. She wasn't about to admit to her father that yes, she had met someone, someone she was having fantastic sex with that she planned on never seeing again once things fizzled out.

"Met someone? No. I did get a full seven hours of sleep last night, though." That was true. She'd been surprised when there was enough of a break at work for her to feel comfortable leaving before dark.

"That must be it, then. Have you thought any more about Thanksgiving?"

"It's going to be a busy time, Daddy." After seeing the sad

look on his face, Olivia tried to mentally rearrange her work calendar to allow for an evening off in late November. She hated Thanksgiving. "But I could probably break away for an evening."

His smile was contagious, and Olivia grinned back at her father.

"Well! That's good because there's someone I want you to meet."

Olivia's smile fell. "Who?"

"Her name is Jeanette. She works at Shady Oaks where I volunteer. She's an exceptional woman."

"I'm sure she is."

"What? Don't hold your tongue, now. I knew you'd have something you wanted to say to me as soon as I mentioned her. So, let's have it." He was amused. Olivia was not.

"I just don't want to see you get hurt. Again."

"I'm not hurting right now."

"And if it doesn't work out with this Jeanette person? Are you going to mope around and feel helpless and lonely?"

"I've never been helpless in my life, Olivia. When your mother left, it's true it was hard."

Olivia sat back, feeling nauseous. She hated him talking about her mother.

"She took with her a few things. One, my signed Led Zeppelin album, and two, my peace of mind. I don't know why your mother was unhappy. I spent years trying to figure it out. What I did wrong. What I could have done differently. But as an old man, I am coming to realize that she left because of her. Not because of me."

Olivia looked at her father. He looked different.

"I realized that with other women, I'd been too focused on how to keep them happy, how to keep them around. That's no way to build a relationship. With Jeanette, it's easy. We're honest with each other, we want the same things, and we enjoy just being together. Can't you see that's what it should be like? I found it. And so will you."

Now Olivia was truly sick. She didn't want to find it. *Find someone perfect and then learn that they aren't?* Find someone she wanted to make a life with only to have them desert her like her mother had? No way. Olivia hated repeating this conversation with her father. With Joan. With herself. Her inability to even want a committed relationship made her feel like some fucked-up teen on *Dr. Phil*, the product of a broken home who couldn't fully trust anyone. It screamed weakness.

Olivia hated it.

Not that she wanted any of that happy ending stuff anyway. Work fueled her and challenged her in a way people didn't. Work she could control, change, and mold the way she wanted. Olivia had yet to find a person so easily managed.

At this thought, a visceral image of Cardic, naked on her knees in front of Olivia, popped to mind. But that was different. Sex was different. That was easy to control.

"Are you still dead set against marriage or a relationship of any kind?"

"Yes."

"So, you'd deny me the chance to be a grandfather? You are my only child. My name will die with you."

"Daddy, don't be dramatic. Uncle Jeremy has four sons."

"And twelve grandkids."

"Daddy, just stop. It's not in the cards for me."

"But how will you know if you don't even play the hand you're dealt?"

"I play," Olivia said in her defense, keeping her eyes trained on the menu to block out another daunting image of Cardic in her bed.

"Olivia, I just want to make sure you aren't avoiding

or pushing things away that have the potential to make you happy."

"Daddy. I am happy. I am happy with you, with work, with my life. I don't need anyone else to make me happy."

"I feel very proud of your successes, and I know you don't need anyone. It doesn't mean you should deny yourself a loving partner because you are so fiercely independent."

For some reason, Olivia felt like the fates were aligned to prove a point. Her old classmate dying of a massive heart attack. Her dad finding true love. Again. And Cardic.

But what about Cardic? They both agreed to the same thing. And the subtle shift in Cardic's features when she read Megan's name, whoever that was, was enough to show her Cardic had her own baggage. And Olivia wanted no part in it. She'd pick her own hand and make her own luck.

Later in the evening, after forcing herself to work and trying to push the conversation with her dad from her mind, Olivia was surprised to find herself curling up on the couch with the TV on. As a rule, she never napped. Sleeping was an annoyance.

After flipping through channels and not landing on anything enticing, she drifted into a restless sleep.

Olivia opened her eyes to the inside of a dream. She looked down at her attire and figured she must be in some sort of period piece from the early 1900s. She rubbed the boning and stitch details in the tight empire-waisted coat and felt the brim of the large hat on top of her head.

A slight shift in her footing made her glance up to the large expanse of water in front of her, no land in sight. A wave of sickness hit her, and she grabbed the railing of what appeared to be a large ship. The dream was slowly turning into a nightmare.

"Olive, this is your dream. Don't let yourself get seasick."

Joan waltzed over in a similarly modest early twentieth-century outfit.

"My dream? What do you mean? And I do not get seasick." Olivia straightened her back, which was easy in this vise of a getup. "Is this the—"

"*Titanic*? Yeah. Hope you wake up before we hit the berg. But come with me; you've gotta see this." Joan grabbed her by the elbow and pulled her farther down the deck of the ship.

Later, Olivia was shocked at the realness and absurdity of her dream because she didn't have any interest in the *Titanic*. She had never even seen the movie.

They rounded a corner, then Joan stopped short and pointed. "Look! Isn't it fabulous?"

"What am I doing here? It's really a dream?" Olivia asked.

Olivia's eyes darted around the huge swimming pool situated in the middle of the deck inside a four-story atrium. Vines and flowers clung to every wall and window, creating a jungle-like feel inside the glass enclosure.

Inside the pool was what appeared to be a synchronized swim team. She watched in awe as they circled the water effortlessly, sticking their legs up, bending their knees in precise symmetry.

They all wore retro swim caps with small flowers on the side above the ear. Their swimsuits were a simple navy one-piece, sporty but not unfashionable.

Olivia's mind switched gears as she contemplated a new retro swimwear line for Vital.

Joan snapped her fingers in front of Olivia's face and sighed. "Even in your dreams you think of work?"

Olivia gasped as strong hands grabbed her waist from behind. She didn't need to turn around. She knew those hands.

"I can help you forget about work," Cardic whispered close to Olivia's ear.

Olivia was afraid to turn around and see Cardic in what was surely to be a jaw-dropping dapper costume. She stared straight ahead at the swimmers, who were disappearing as time wore on. Come to think of it, Joan was gone now, too.

Olivia held her breath and turned around. There stood Cardic in a top hat and velvet coat, with a pinstriped shirt and polka dot suspenders underneath. Olivia searched her beautiful face, trying to control the slight shake of her hands and the whoosh of her anxious breath. Olivia ran her hands inside the soft velvet to feel the muscles of Cardic's chest and sighed. This was a dream, after all, wasn't it? She could do just as she pleased, and no one would be the wiser.

As she started to speak, Cardic kissed her. "I know what you're going to say. Something about control. But, Olivia, don't you understand yet?"

Olivia shook her head, afraid of what Cardic would say next.

Cardic wore a predatory grin and dipped her head to capture Olivia's lips again. "No one's in control of this."

Just as Cardic's lips almost met hers, Olivia jerked awake to her cold, dark apartment.

❖

"Auntie Cardic, let's play superheroes. I want to be Spider-Man."

"Oh yeah? Can I be Batman?"

"Yeah. And for Hall'ween I'm gonna be Spider-Man. With a Batmobile."

Clark toddled over to a large cardboard box that served as his Batmobile. After organizing some of her data notebooks, Cardic had brought over the empty box, and she and Clark spent a Saturday together turning it into a homemade superhero car.

One of Cardic's favorite things about Clark was his imagination. He could easily turn an empty box into a car, a toilet paper roll into a spyglass, or Play-Doh into hair for his G.I. Joe. Clark reminded her so much of her sister. He was sweet and gentle and rarely shouted as so many young kids do. Often when she took Clark out on one of their dates, people would comment on his excellent behavior. As Clark pulled his Spider-Man beanie on, Cardic smiled, picturing him running around in a Spider-Man costume with a Batman cape.

"You've been doing that a lot lately," Claire said as she brought in a large basketful of clean laundry. One of the many reasons Cardic reminded herself kids were a bad idea was the never-ending laundry that came with the territory.

"What have I been doing? Knocking over block towers?"

"Smiling, you idiot."

Cardic debated how to approach this as she propped her head up on her fist, lying on her side on the carpet. Play into the "you're so happy, what's going on" line of questioning, or just be honest. Slightly honest. As in "I've met a woman I'm sleeping with" and leaving out the sordid details and the nasty fact that they shared zero emotional connection and actually kind of annoyed each other.

"I'm finally diving into my data. It's amazing to see it all come together."

Claire looked skeptical. "Data. Your one and only true love."

"Speaking of love, did Dad tell you he's bailing on our golf trip?"

"Ha! I'm sure you're crushed."

Cardic tolerated golfing with her dad once a year in Palm

Springs because it gave her mother the impression they had some semblance of a relationship.

"He's going to Bali."

"Yay! That frees you up to spend Thanksgiving with us." Claire looked at Clark, who was now stacking blocks in front of Cardic. "Umm, D-A-D wants to see you-know-who on Thanksgiving this year."

Cardic took a deep breath, suppressing the urge to throw something, before responding. "You could just spell 'asshole,' then I'd know immediately who you're talking about."

"Auntie, that's a potty word."

"Sorry, buddy."

"Yeah, *Auntie.* Watch your mouth."

Cardic stared at her in astonishment. "Are you actually considering granting that request?"

Claire glanced at Clark, then down at her hands.

"Claire." Cardic jumped up and came to sit at her side. "When was the last time he paid child support?"

She hesitated. "June."

Knowing the situation was difficult for her sister, Cardic tried to be patient. "Maybe he should be paid up before he offers to babysit."

"Cardic," Claire said. This was always a dangerous topic for them. Claire was always defensive, and Cardic always wanted to throttle the shit stick.

"I'm sorry. I just don't want him around Clark."

"We'll continue this later."

Claire abandoned the laundry and scooped Clark up before heading to the living room, where Cardic figured Clark would make them watch the same Spider-Man DVD they'd already watched twice.

After the little man fell asleep against Claire's chest, she whispered, "I regret everything I did for him, except giving him a child. Just look at him." Claire stroked Clark's soft little cheek and kissed the top of his head. "I know I don't owe him anything. But nothing he did to me, the cheating, the lying, nothing takes away my gratitude for Clark. I'm sorry. I know how you feel about him."

Cardic reached for her hand and held it, amazed at her sister's moral fiber and character. "I wish I was as good a person as you are. I just don't want you to go through any more than you already have where he's concerned."

"I think we're really getting ahead of ourselves. He probably won't even follow through. But I'd rather Clark have some kind of relationship with him than feel the way you do about Dad."

Cardic had to admit the resentment and tension she felt with her father she wouldn't wish on anyone else.

"Then let's just play it by ear. We'll talk about Thanksgiving after his birthday."

"Are you ready for the party? He's so excited you're going to be there."

"Of course I'll be there. I wouldn't miss it."

Chapter Fourteen

"Olivia, Howard's on line three."

Olivia grabbed her phone receiver and held it to her shoulder as she finished typing an email. "Reynolds."

"Hey, Olivia, it's Howard."

Howard worked for Vital on a contract basis and moderated all of their focus groups. He was all business and not particularly warm and fuzzy—similar to Olivia.

"Do you have some good news for me?"

"Actually, yes. The focus group went great. After the initial participants that you approved, we moved forward on Monday and met for about an hour and a half. You'll have a hard copy of my report tomorrow morning, but I went ahead and sent you an email."

"Excellent. So, what was the response?" Olivia wanted to hear how her fellow plus-size consumers reacted to the "Love Life" line of supportive plus-size sports bras. After her meeting with Melissa last week, Olivia promised if the scheduled focus group didn't go well, she'd abandon the whole line. As a DD herself, Olivia knew how difficult it could be to find the right sports bra, the right any kind of bra. She believed in the product and wanted to see it as part of the Vital relaunch.

"The response was overwhelmingly positive. We had one concern about the fabric stretching over time, but after finding out we use the same double-stitch Lycra as with all of our other athletic wear, Melissa seemed convinced as well."

"Fabulous. Howard, I owe you a drink."

After sending a salty email to Melissa with Howard's email attached, Olivia decided to call Cardic. Now that she knew there was one less thing on her plate, she wanted to jump at the chance to spend time with her.

Sleep with Cardic. Sleep *with her.*

When she didn't answer, Olivia left a voice mail. It was four o'clock on Wednesday, and Cardic taught a two-hour lecture class on Monday and Wednesday. "Hey, it's me. I got some good news at work. It's really going to cut down on my workload for the next few days." Olivia turned her chair toward the window and lowered her voice. "I want to see you. Let me know if you're free tonight."

Olivia was pleased she didn't have to wait long for a text from Cardic agreeing to meet her at a little French bakery right off the Blue Line in Bucktown. After the initial excitement and high from the good news from Howard wore off, Olivia grew more tense. She'd be tempted by two of her weaknesses tonight: French pastries and Dr. Cardic Lawson.

❖

"No, Doc, look, when they bury the men, they only use the palm fronds. They don't use the flowers of the plant, and they also don't bury plants with the body."

"See this photo of when we buried Muap? They used the purple flowers here. Why? They didn't with any of the other male burials I showed you pictures from." Cardic flipped through several different photos she had taken of burial ceremonies of the Yanapo.

"No, I'm telling you, I've looked through them all. He's the only one with flowers."

Cardic ran her hands through her hair. She needed another trim. It was falling into her eyes much too often.

In all her observations, Cardic had noted the types of plants and objects present at the burial ceremonies. Unlike some neighboring tribes, the Yanapo buried their dead rather than cremating them.

After looking through her notes on the burials, a pattern emerged. Except one funeral, only women were buried with local flowers. The graves of the men were lined with rocks and covered with palm fronds. But the women were buried with flowers, dolls, as well as bowls made from sticks and local plants, painted rocks. Why had this one tribesman been buried with flowers and none of the other men while she'd been there?

"Damnit!" Cardic threw her notebook across the room. If only she were still in the jungle and could pull her tribesman aside and ask them why things were done this way. "Why didn't I see this before? Why is the ceremony so different for men and women, except for Muap?"

"Hey, remember what you say to the kids in Intro to Observational Methods, it doesn't matter why. It only matters that it happens."

Cardic gave Patrick a dirty look as she bent to retrieve her scattered notes. "Yeah, yeah."

Glancing at a picture of Muap's funeral, Cardic noticed for the first time a young woman in the picture with the other funeral goers. She held a small bouquet of the local purple flowers, tears running down her face. She looked younger than Muap by at least a decade. A sister, perhaps? There were eighty-nine members of this Yanapo tribe when Cardic left the

Amazon, and she was ashamed to admit she didn't know them all by name.

"Who is this?" Cardic pointed at her face and held the picture out for Patrick.

"I think she lives in *yano* number seven, with Insa and Yalop and five of the children." Patrick walked over to the large map of the tribal area and pointed to one of the yanos. "I'll have to double-check. Her name starts with T."

Cardic's head was starting to pound, and all she wanted to do was crawl between Olivia's legs to ease the tension all over her body. Cardic glanced at the clock as she packed up her laptop. Leaving now would put her in Bucktown a little early, but she was ready to be off campus. "I'll see you tomorrow. Text me if you remember her name."

❖

When Olivia walked into Petite Gâteau about an hour later, a warm tingle ran over Cardic's entire body. Olivia didn't see her at first, so she watched her carefully scan the restaurant, her brows knitted in concentration. She was dressed in a form-hugging black dress with a soft pink cardigan on top. The woman looked amazing in black. And pink. And naked. A small brown belt wrapped around her middle and accentuated her tiny waist. Cardic's mouth watered. She raised her hand and waved to get Olivia's attention.

"Hey." Olivia looked down at the table, flooded with notes and pictures, concern showing on her face. "Are you too busy for tonight? We can meet another time." She hesitated to sit down.

"No, no, please sit. I just got here early and needed to go over some files."

Olivia peered at the papers and photos scattered all

over the table. Her hand brushed the stack of photos and her questioning eyes met Cardic's. "May I?"

"Please do."

As Olivia's gentle hands held the photos and her bright green eyes scanned the images with interest, Cardic wished they were alone. She wanted to shove her notes to the floor and jump across the table at Olivia like some kind of animal. She felt antsy and wild. Her annoyance from the workday fueled her already high sex drive. Cardic glanced at the clock and hoped Olivia wouldn't want to stay long.

"This is where you lived?"

Cardic nodded.

"What's this?" Olivia pointed to the photo of Muap's funeral that she and Patrick had agonized over all afternoon. Olivia's bright, curious eyes darted all over the photo.

"That was a burial of a tribesman named Muap. He was bitten by a snake. When the shaman was unable to treat him, he died from the wound."

Suddenly looking sad, Olivia continued to flip through the photos. "How many people died while you were there?"

"Seven. And eleven were born. The Yanapo don't grieve their dead very long. But the life of a newborn is celebrated for months." Cardic took the pile of photos and flipped through until she found the one she was looking for. "They make blankets for the baby out of soft leaves, dolls out of sticks, they even make them little jewelry." Cardic remembered the love and solidarity created by the birth of a baby in the tribe, and her spirits lifted.

As Cardic explained more about the many different traditions when a baby was born into the Yanapo, Olivia lost track of her words. Her strong fingers pointed things out in the photos, but Olivia's eyes were pulled to her tan forearms, muscles tensing with her movements. Her full lips were moving and words were coming out, yet Olivia couldn't hear anything except her own heartbeat.

"I'm sorry, what did you say?"

Cardic gave her a knowing smile. "I asked if you wanted a pastry or coffee."

Olivia caressed Cardic's hand on top of the table. "To go?" Her voice sounded husky even to her own ears.

"Yes. Go order. I'll pack all this up. Meet you at the front?"

Olivia was surprised at the urge to call Cardic by some lame pet name and kiss her on the cheek as she stood. Olivia planned out their evening in bed as she headed to the counter. Giving orders for Cardic to please her should remove any weird and unwelcome thoughts of lovey-dovey name-calling.

The cab ride was tense in the best possible way. They decided to go to Cardic's place since it was closer. As they climbed the stairs to Cardic's apartment, Olivia could hardly contain her excitement. She'd been thinking about Cardic all day. She just wanted to touch her and taste her everywhere.

"Let me just toss this in the fridge. Make yourself comfortable."

Comfortable she would be. Olivia kicked off her heels as she entered Cardic's bedroom and ran her hands over the soft down comforter. She remembered Cardic telling her it'd been difficult to get used to such luxuries when she returned home.

Olivia took off her jewelry and placed it on the bedside table, turning on the lamp.

"I can't decide if I like you better naked or in your clothes. You're so beautiful."

Just the sound of Cardic's voice made Olivia wet. Olivia dropped her light sweater, still facing away from her. "Well, it's time for naked. Can you unzip me, please?"

"With pleasure." Cardic gently moved Olivia's bouncy

curls to her left shoulder and placed her lips just above the clasp of her dress.

Olivia held on to the night table and prayed for the strength to make this last.

With unbearable slowness, Cardic unzipped her dress and revealed the smooth skin of Olivia's back. She pushed the material away from her shoulders and down, then moved forward so their bodies were flush.

"Take your clothes off and lie down on the bed."

Cardic complied, annoyed at having to move away from Olivia's warm skin. She got on the bed and laced her fingers behind her head.

Olivia removed her dress and underwear and walked toward the bed. Cardic's hips lifted slightly at the sway of Olivia's hips, the way she trailed her hands up and down her ribs as she got nearer.

The feeling of Olivia's wetness against her stomach as she straddled her was enough to drive Cardic mad. She let out a long breath. All she wanted to do was flip her over and ride her until they came together. But she couldn't. Instead she ran her hands up and down Olivia's thighs, squeezing and kneading the soft flesh.

"Now," Olivia's voice was strained and breathy, "you're going to come. When I do. Not before. Do you understand?"

Cardic nodded with force, keeping her eyes closed. If she couldn't *see* Olivia's naked body, maybe she could slow down.

"You can touch me anywhere." Olivia thrust her hips, moving down until her center met with Cardic's. "But you cannot come until I do."

Given permission, Cardic reached for Olivia's right breast as she continued to rub her hip and thigh with the other hand.

She knew Olivia loved to have her nipples pinched, so she pulled until Olivia let out a moan.

Between the sound of Olivia's voice and the feeling of her body moving against her, Cardic wasn't going to last much longer. Cardic ran a hand up Olivia's chest to caress her face and rubbed her bottom lip with her thumb. She felt Olivia's tongue dart out and pushed her thumb inside Olivia's warm mouth until she sucked.

"Fuck. Olivia, I can't. I'm going to come."

Olivia's hips grew more insistent, and she pulled at Cardic's shoulders, digging her dark red nails into her skin.

Cardic pulled her thumb from the heat of Olivia's mouth and trailed her wet finger down her chest and stomach. When she reached Olivia's clit and rubbed back and forth a few times, Olivia's head fell back, and Cardic could feel her muscles tense.

"Yes, yes. Come now, Cardic. Come now."

Cardic ground her teeth and lifted Olivia's body with her hips to increase the pressure. It started slow, but in no time heat flooded her center and Cardic exploded.

"My God, that was fantastic." Olivia squeezed Cardic's biceps as she stretched and mewled like a kitten.

"I've been thinking about that since the last time I saw you."

Olivia covered her face and groaned. "God, I feel like I'm thinking about it all the time."

The comment surprised Cardic. Olivia didn't usually say much about what she was thinking. "I was trying not to sound like a horny teenager, but yeah, me, too. Even during class. My God, I just can't get you out of my head."

"During class?" Olivia moved some fiery red curls away from her face and snuggled closer to Cardic, licking her damp neck and squeezing her breasts. "What on earth do you think about during class?"

"Honestly?"

"Honestly."

"Topping you. How hot it would be." Cardic could feel Olivia smiling against her skin. She tried to keep her voice even as Olivia's hand moved down her stomach, teasing and caressing.

"But those weren't the rules you specified. Remember, Dr. Lawson?"

Cardic moaned as Olivia entered her with one swift stroke. "Oh, the rules. Right. What's that…that saying about rules? They're meant to be broken?" The skill of Olivia's hands and tongue made it almost impossible to think, let alone carry on a conversation.

"But you're so sexy this way. Open. Responsive. Submissive." Olivia punctuated each word with a tug or caress. She was learning exactly what Cardic needed to get off, and exactly when to back off so she couldn't.

Cardic forgot the conversation, forgot the agreement, forgot everything except this siren next to her, and she relented. She leaned back and grabbed a fistful of the sheet, moaning and thrashing until Olivia delivered her when she wanted to.

Chapter Fifteen

"What was Muap like?"

Olivia didn't flinch when Cardic took her hand as she walked her to the train station. Cardic didn't know if this was against the rules, but it just felt right to touch Olivia all the time. Whenever she could. "He was very strong and quiet. His name means 'night bird' because he didn't sleep very much. He was the tallest male in the tribe. Sometimes he would play with the kids and carry three or four of them around at the same time to show off."

Olivia smiled brightly, that same real smile Cardic had seen when she gave her the pumpkin. Only this time, she didn't try to hide it. Her eyes lit up, and her teeth showed. Cardic almost had to stop walking to just stare at her. But she knew Olivia would back away. And whatever this slight change in dynamic was, Cardic welcomed it.

"Did they give you a name?"

Cardic ran a hand through her hair. She hated this question. But why should she be embarrassed? It was her rightful Yanapo name, and she was proud of it. But the double entendre was hard to escape. "Yako gave me a name. He was one of my favorite tribesmen. I spent a lot of time with him. After I'd been with the tribe about two weeks, they kept saying

'Keylek.' In my study of the language before arriving there I'd never heard that word, but there were many words I didn't know yet. Anyway, finally, I realized they were referring to me by this word, so I asked Yako what it meant."

Olivia's smile widened, and she pulled at Cardic's hand. "And?"

"They said my head seemed like a pile of dirt before a storm, desperate for water and absorbing anything it could get. I asked a lot of questions. Apparently, more than the last anthropologist who visited. 'Keylek' roughly translated means 'dirty mind.'"

Olivia stopped and covered her mouth with her hand, hiding a girlish giggle. Cardic stopped and looked down at her.

"They must have known you better than I thought."

"Oh, come on. My mind isn't that dirty."

"No? Didn't you just tell me you think about me during class?" Olivia leaned back against a wrought iron gate in front of a modern-looking two flat.

"Well, what do you think about at work? Just work?"

Olivia tried to keep her easy smile in place. Work was easy. It was the easiest and most predictable thing in her life. She didn't like or welcome the distracting thoughts of Cardic that had been invading her mind. And not just sexual thoughts. Thoughts about what she was doing during the day. Thoughts about what kind of a teacher she was. Thoughts about what it would be like to come home to her.

Deciding to distract Cardic with sex, Olivia slid her arm around Cardic's waist and pulled her close. "Sometimes work. Sometimes you. Sometimes I think about fucking you in my office." Olivia ran her tongue down Cardic's throat and felt her squirm and try to back away.

"Come on, your train's coming."

"Fine, fine. Just thought I'd get one for the road."

"I can't make you come right in the middle of Sheridan Avenue."

"Can't or won't? I thought I made the rules."

Cardic always rose to a challenge, but she wasn't about to get arrested. Although she could play along. Cardic wore a fierce expression as she slowly moved her hand up Olivia's waist until her hand was almost at her breast. "I think we both know I *can* make you come anytime I want to."

Cardic extended her thumb to gently rub Olivia's nipple through her shirt until her eyes closed with a moan.

"But you'll have to wait."

"Tease."

"This weekend?"

"Oh, most definitely."

❖

"Hey, stranger." Joan tossed her yoga mat into the grass and sat next to Olivia. When either of them missed working out or needed to relieve some stress, they'd switch their lunch dates for workouts instead. It was Joan's turn to pick. Olivia wasn't too fond of yoga but loved being in a studio with large windows and a view of the lake. "Your new lady love must be spectacular in bed."

That's an understatement. "Why do you ask?"

"I called you twice this week at the office, and you weren't in." Joan stretched out her left leg and bent to touch her toes, not making eye contact with Olivia. It was her usual tactic when trying to get Olivia to talk.

Olivia tried to play dumb. "I was in all week. With things so busy, I haven't really been taking calls."

"From me? Bullshit. But it's fine. I'll be ready to talk when you are."

"Ready to talk about what?"

"You've spent more time with this woman in the past few weeks than any woman I've ever seen you with."

Olivia stared at the shimmery water of the lake and prayed for an answer that made sense as she slid into a downward dog pose. "We do not even see each other that much. Maybe once a week. And you were right. The sex has been a great stress reliever."

Joan wore a smug expression and seemed content to be right for a change since Olivia always made a point of being right. Maybe that stroke to her ego would keep her questions at bay. Olivia didn't want to examine things. She just wanted to feel. The feelings Cardic awoke in her were unlike anything she'd ever experienced. But it was just sex. Just sex.

"Sal will be in town next weekend. Maybe we could all get together." Sal was Joan's on-again, off-again boyfriend. Right now, they were on.

"No. No way." Olivia was horrified at the idea of going out socially with Cardic. They were only sleeping together. No meeting friends or families. No commitments. Just sex.

"What? Why? It's only natural. I'm sleeping with Sal. You're sleeping with Cardic. We all have to eat. Let's just get together for a meal before we have sex."

Olivia was getting irritated. It was one thing if Joan wanted her to have an outlet for stress, but trying to manipulate and railroad her into some makeshift relationship was crossing a line. "Joan, I appreciate your concern for my stress level, but right now the only thing causing me stress is you."

"Olive, what's with the attitude? I just thought it'd be fun."

"No, you thought me and Cardic being with you and Sal on some kind of double date will get the relationship sparks flying. It's just an affair, Joan. That's it. Just butt out."

"I know it's just an affair. I'm starting to wonder if you know that."

Olivia straightened and stared at Joan, flabbergasted. "Excuse me?"

"Olive. Let's just cut the shit. Every time I bring up Cardic you get defensive and weird. Way weirder than you'd get if you were just fucking someone. And I'm not saying I want you to be in a relationship or fall in love. I'd honestly pity the woman who thought she could compete with your career." Joan turned to Olivia and gave her a sympathetic smile. "I know you're not honest with me about how you feel about her. Which is fine. We've been friends for a long time. I know how you are. But I think this time, I also know you're not being honest with yourself."

❖

Claire's house was nestled on an adorable street in Andersonville. Huge trees lined the streets and there were children's toys in almost every one of the small front yards. Olivia resisted the urge to straighten her shirt before ringing the doorbell when she arrived at Claire's address.

When Cardic declined her offer to spend Saturday together, Olivia was disappointed. They hadn't been together since Wednesday, and they'd seen each other every Saturday since their affair began. During a moment of sheer insanity, Olivia wondered if it had something to do with Cardic's old colleague, Megan. The one who had called and left her a message. But then Olivia reminded herself it really didn't matter why Cardic couldn't see her Saturday.

"My nephew. It's his birthday party," Cardic had said when Olivia stayed quiet on the phone, trying to hold her tongue.

"Oh, that sounds like fun," Olivia replied.

"Ha, no, it doesn't. But I really want to see you. Why don't you swing by the party and we can leave together from there? It'll be a good excuse for me to dip out early. I'll buy you dinner."

"And what about dessert?" Olivia could hear Cardic's breathing change. She imagined Cardic in her office, getting wet, trying to hide her arousal. "What if I want dessert before dinner?"

"Your wish is my command."

Yes. This was what Olivia wanted. Husky voice, rapid breaths, Cardic reduced to a ball of need. No talk of double dates or families or anything else Olivia had worked so hard in her life to avoid. Just the intense pleasure of two women racing to the peak of physical desire together.

But somehow, here she stood now, with a wrapped Spider-Man toy from the dollar store down the street, about to enter a house full of domestic poison.

Before she could muster the courage to knock, the door opened and a small clone of Cardic stood there wearing a Spider-Man T-shirt.

"Your hair is red. Like Spider-Man's suit," the child said with excitement as he poked out his chest and pointed to his shirt.

"Not quite the same shade, buddy."

As Olivia saw Cardic behind the door, she wondered if the fluttery feeling in her stomach every time their eyes met was a permanent thing or something that would eventually wear off. Olivia wondered if she looked overdressed in her pencil skirt, blazer, and billowy scarf as she took in Cardic's black Spider-Man T-shirt.

Olivia had never mastered the goochie-goochie goo voice. She bent down so she could look the child in the eye and handed over the present. In her very regular voice she said, "Hi, Clark. This is for you. Happy birthday."

Cardic watched Olivia interact with her nephew, her head tilted to the side, a gentle expression on her face. She was reminded of the day a baby boy had been born during her field study. Yako was there along with several other female tribespeople and the shaman. Men weren't forbidden from attending a birthing ceremony, but it was rare.

Yako had watched intently as the baby was pushed from his mother's body, too hypnotized to look away. It was the second birth Cardic had been present for, the first being Clark's. In both instances, she been so overcome with emotion that she felt tears on her face though she hadn't been aware she had been crying.

As an anthropologist, Cardic understood the importance of family and kinship. And until very recently, she thought Claire and Clark were enough of a family for her. Not that she wanted a wife or a child, but she just felt...incomplete. Something was missing, and she needed to figure out what. At least she had Cicero.

And sex. Lots of sex.

After her discussion with Clark, Olivia rose and glanced around with a nervous expression. Cardic assumed she was worried this might look like a date or a relationship when nothing could be further from the truth. "My family knows me better than to make assumptions. No worries."

Cardic held out her hand for Olivia to precede her into the hallway. "We're all just in the backyard."

The cozy living room opened up to the back of the house with an updated kitchen. There were pictures of Clark and Cardic everywhere, as well as more of her dark-haired, brown-eyed family. Clark's artwork littered the fridge, and there was an array of finger foods and cupcakes on the large island.

"Your sister has a lovely home."

"She'll be happy to hear that. She renovated it herself. With little help from her loser ex-husband."

The backyard seemed large for such a small home. A large privacy fence hid the yard from the neighbor's view, and large trees and bushes lined the perimeter. There was a small swing set in the back and a picnic table with more snacks and juice boxes. Olivia glanced around at all the adults talking and laughing in small groups. Then she noticed only a few children.

"Clark had a very specific guest list. Only the kids in his preschool class that like Spider-Man were invited. So cliquish, I know!"

As Olivia continued to scan the yard, a petite woman who resembled Cardic bounced over in a pink Spider-Man shirt.

"You must be Olivia." Claire smiled a bright, genuine smile, and Olivia couldn't help but smile back.

"Thank you for having me."

Cardic elbowed Olivia in the ribs and whispered, "Don't tell the birthday boy, but she's more of a Batman fan."

Claire gave a mock look of horror, then pinched Cardic's arm. "Be nice. Or the only woman you've ever brought over will leave before she gets a cupcake."

Olivia tried to hide her shock. But why be shocked? Cardic didn't do relationships either, so it was no wonder she'd never brought a woman over. Olivia trusted Cardic at her word that there would be no assumptions made, so she tried to play it cool. "I love cupcakes." Olivia winked at Cardic in the hopes it would ease any nervousness. This was her family and her turf. Olivia would feel extremely awkward introducing a lover to her family.

After walking around for a few minutes and meeting some of Clark's friends and their parents, Cardic pointed to a bench in the corner of the yard surrounded by green hydrangeas. "Would you like a drink?"

"Anything but a juice box."

With her signature grin in place, Cardic backed away and headed for the cooler.

Taking her eyes off Cardic's body was hard. Olivia felt guilty for feeling the tingle in her core when she was sitting at a child's birthday party. As she got to the cooler, Clark ran over and hugged Cardic's leg. As Cardic bent to pick him up, Olivia swallowed a moan at the sight of Cardic's biceps flexing and her corded muscles moving under her smooth skin.

"Hello, my dear! You must be Olivia!"

And you are Cardic's mother.

Olivia stood to greet the woman who was practically galloping over to her. Her face resembled Cardic's, but her small, compact body reminded Olivia more of Claire.

"I'm wearing my Vital walking sandals. I pretty much wear them everywhere. It's such a pleasure to meet you. Thank you so much for coming. I'm sure you can't stay long. I'm Katherine." The woman pushed flowing brown waves out of her face and stuck out her hand to shake Olivia's.

"Well, I'm so pleased you like the sandals. Our new line is launching soon. I hope you can find something you like as much." Thank God the woman brought up Vital. Nothing made Olivia less nervous than talking about work.

Katherine studied Olivia's face and smiled brightly before glancing back and calling across the yard, "Cardic, darling, do come here."

Cardic finished the brief conversation with a young man and turned toward them. When Cardic noticed her mother standing there, she gave Olivia an apologetic look and rushed through the yard with a beer bottle in each hand.

"Yes, Mother?" Cardic inserted herself between them as if trying to shield Olivia from her rather pleasant mother.

"Tell me, dear, where did you meet this breathtaking redhead?"

"Funny, that's what I call her."

Cardic gave Olivia a sexy grin as she sipped from her beer bottle. It reminded Olivia of the first time they slept together, when she had teased Cardic's nipples with the cool glass. If Olivia thought it was possible, she'd guess she was blushing. It just wasn't right to get turned on by someone in front of their mother and at a child's birthday party.

"We met at the lake. Olivia almost ran me over, then begged me to take her to dinner."

"Oh, please. You chased me for weeks until I gave in so you'd quit annoying me."

Katherine seemed interested in the tale of their meeting, but suddenly Cardic's eyes were riveted to the large plate glass window at the back of the house.

"And when was the first date?" Katherine asked.

If Olivia hadn't been so preoccupied with the look of hatred on Cardic's face, she would have been horrified at the mention of her and Cardic "dating."

"Just a few weeks ago," Olivia said, trying to keep the conversation going as she followed Cardic's line of sight. Claire was in the kitchen speaking with a man Olivia hadn't seen when they arrived.

"Excuse me," Cardic snarled, heading with purpose through the throng of children and into the back door of the house.

"Maybe it's the guacamole. My Cardic has always had a weak stomach." Katherine gave a giggle as she gestured for Olivia to join her on the bench. Apparently, Katherine had not noticed the unwanted newcomer.

Katherine asked Olivia more questions about Vital and the new line. To her relief, Olivia could answer anything about Vital in her sleep, so she could continue to concentrate on what Cardic was getting herself into.

After exchanging a quick word with her sister, Cardic attempted to walk toward the man, but Claire blocked her way. Her hands on Cardic's shoulders, Claire appeared to be pleading with Cardic. Cardic turned around abruptly and threw her fist at the wall before walking out of the back door, letting it slam behind her.

At the look of contempt and rage on Cardic's face, Olivia rose as she walked across the yard, waiting for Cardic to tell her what to do or where to go. Katherine stood as well when she saw Cardic approach.

"Cardic, what on earth..." Katherine's voice trailed off as she looked behind Cardic toward the house. "He wasn't supposed to be here. I'm sorry, darling."

Looking into Olivia's eyes, Cardic gave a tight nod and said, "Let's go."

Chapter Sixteen

The train ride back to Olivia's apartment was tense. Olivia didn't say much because she didn't want to stick her nose where it didn't belong. She and Cardic were sleeping together, not providing emotional support for family drama. Though she was curious what could put such a scowl on that beautiful face. What could cause this relaxed, carefree woman to act with such aggression? Olivia had never punched a wall. She'd thrown things as a child, but her father put an end to that quickly. Anger never turned physical.

"Would you like something to eat? I have some leftover Thai. I'm also an excellent sandwich maker," Olivia said as she switched on the kitchen light and opened the fridge.

"No, I ate at the party. Thanks, though. But you go ahead if you're hungry."

Cardic's voice still sounded gruff, as if a ball of anger was lodged in her throat. As Cardic washed her hands in the sink, Olivia noticed the bloody scrapes across her knuckles.

"You're hurt." Olivia was startled by the blood dripping into the white porcelain sink. How had she not noticed it on the train? "You've been bleeding this whole time?"

"Well, I wrapped it in a Spider-Man napkin." Cardic gave a lopsided grin, some humor back in her dark eyes.

"Come here." Olivia grabbed Cardic's arm and held it between her own arm and her ribs, gently washing away the blood as Cardic stood right behind her.

Too curious to stop herself, Olivia asked, "What, did he steal your girlfriend?"

No. My girlfriend's right here.

Cardic was shocked at the thought as it passed through her mind. Where the hell did that come from? She winced as Olivia applied a small amount of pressure to her hand. "No, that was David. My sister's ex. And Clark's very deadbeat dad."

Olivia made a sound of understanding in the back of her throat. Something about that sound and her arm nestled against Olivia's curves started a tingle in her belly. Cardic could spend the rest of the evening seething in anger about the nerve of David to show up at Clark's birthday party. She could spend the rest of the night appalled at her sister's and mother's lack of backbone when it came to that man. Or she could spend the next few blissful hours taking orders from Olivia about how to make her come.

As Olivia toweled off her hand with care, Cardic wondered what it would be like to have Olivia care for her. To want to be with her in a non-physical, emotional way. Pushing the thought out of her mind, she concentrated on the swell of Olivia's breasts under her blouse.

"I don't think you need a bandage. The bleeding stopped." Olivia squealed as Cardic picked her up by the hips and placed her bottom on the counter.

"You think I'll have full use of the hand tonight, Dr. Reynolds?"

Olivia's sexy seductive smile slid into place, and she wrapped her arms around Cardic's neck. "Why yes, I do, Dr. Lawson."

Cardic was used to being referred to by her title, but for some reason, coming from Olivia's crimson lips, it was more of a turn-on than anything she could recall in recent memory, "Then by all means, lead the way."

Olivia sauntered down the hallway with Cardic on her heels, dropping items of clothing as she went.

"I love this color on you," Cardic said as she pulled at the lavender scarf around Olivia's neck, wanting to see her naked.

Olivia backed away out of reach and unzipped her skirt, then let it fall to the floor. She removed her button-down and bra and kicked off her heels. Olivia stood in her black panties with only the sheer scarf covering her nipples.

Cardic groaned aloud.

"Glad you like it. I have to admit, I've been thinking about *you* and this scarf all day," Olivia said.

Cardic quirked a brow and began to undress. "Not really my style."

Olivia pulled one end of the scarf until it dangled from her hand, exposing her breasts.

Finally seeing Olivia almost naked for the first time in what felt like days, Cardic would agree to anything. "I'll wear it to the Cubs' next playoffs game if you'll just take those panties off."

Olivia lifted an eyebrow, and Cardic worried about what a painful game she was in store for.

"You want to see me without my panties on?" Olivia said in a sickeningly sweet voice as she took the three steps to close the distance between them. "I'm very sorry, Dr. Lawson, but you won't be seeing much." Olivia reached up and tied the scarf around Cardic's eyes, blindfolding her, then she backed away.

If Cardic concentrated hard enough, she knew she could sense where Olivia was, but for some reason all she could concentrate on was her smell. She could smell the perfume on Olivia's scarf, the subtle scent of her room, even her arousal.

"Tell me what you feel," Olivia whispered from behind.

Cardic wasted no time answering. "Hot. Trapped—in a good way. Ready."

Olivia drew lines and shapes on the skin of Cardic's back as she sidled closer, dipping her fingers inside the waistband of Cardic's boxer shorts. "You may remove these."

Cardic complied, taking a step toward the bed. "Olivia, I'm going to fall over."

Olivia gave Cardic a shove until she toppled onto the bed, then Olivia straddled her hips and Cardic braced herself for the warmth of having Olivia pressed against her. Cardic knew better than to touch Olivia without asking, so she obediently stretched her arms out on the bed, waiting to be told what to do.

"And now? What do you feel now?" Olivia's voice was low and quiet.

"I want you. I want you pressed against me. I want you to kiss me."

Cardic contemplated begging for her touch as Olivia's hair fanned her face. She was well past the point of desperation and was not too proud to admit her agony.

"Very well," Olivia whispered as she settled herself firmly against Cardic's body, covering every inch she could reach. Then finally, finally, her lips met Cardic's in a hungry kiss.

Cardic couldn't help herself as she reached for Olivia's ass and squeezed. Judging by the roll of Olivia's hips, that move wasn't against the rules. Cardic tried in vain to hold back and stifled a deep groan as a powerful orgasm ripped through her. Olivia followed close behind, shouting Cardic's name.

Hours later, wrapped naked in each other's arms, Cardic

fought the urge to curl up and sleep. She'd come twice and worked Olivia until she begged her to stop. Exhaustion threatened to claim her.

Olivia's gentle fingers traced the outline of her tattoo, and Cardic shivered. The skin there was still sensitive, and she didn't know if it would ever feel the same. Or if she wanted it to.

"Did it hurt?" Olivia's voice sounded sleepy.

"Like hell. But it was worth it. The Yanapo don't usually mark outsiders. And this particular placement is usually reserved for the men." Cardic grinned down at Olivia in the dim light. "But they thought I was tough."

"You and your dirty mind." Olivia's body shook as she giggled. "Do you miss it?"

"Every day." Some days, Cardic felt the jungle was more her home than this place.

"Will you go back someday?"

"I hope to eventually. I'm not sure when the opportunity will arise. And now with my position being threatened at Loyola, I don't think it will be anytime soon."

"Your position?" Olivia sat up and stared down at Cardic holding the sheet against her breasts. "Is everything all right?"

Cardic felt a concern from Olivia that she hadn't before. The alarm on Olivia's face, her auburn brows knitted together, the gentle hand on her arm. A concern appeared that she shouldn't feel from a detached lover. A wish for her well-being that felt too good and too beyond the physical.

"It'll work itself out. I gotta run." Cardic attempted to act casual and pulled on her T-shirt.

"Yeah, okay. Well, thanks for inviting me to the party. And the display of macho bullshit."

Cardic tossed a pillow at Olivia as she got out of the

bed. Olivia stretched and made a small mewling sound as she adjusted her pillows, apparently not intending to walk Cardic to the door.

Cardic couldn't pull her eyes away from Olivia's full hips and rounded ass. The way she moved her body and didn't care if Cardic saw every inch of it. Her confidence and sexuality were breathtaking. "God, you're beautiful."

Olivia moaned and pulled the sheet up over her. "Go away. Or I'll want you again."

"I'll lock the door behind me. Let me know when you are free next week." As she bent to give Olivia a kiss, Cardic wondered if this was what it would be like. Saying good-bye to someone in the morning. Kissing them and wishing them a good day at work.

When Olivia heard the door close, she tossed the covers off and sat up on her bed, running her hands through her mass of curls. There were many things Olivia wanted in life. Career success. Friends. Hobbies. Travel. But until this very moment, she'd never wanted to sleep next to a woman she'd just had sex with.

After sex, even if Olivia was naked, she felt trapped and suffocated. Once the pleasure of release wore off, she wanted her partner to fade from her mind like a boring novel, one you finish just to get to the end.

Olivia wrapped up in her robe and headed to her patio. She stared at the roofs of the neighboring buildings, wishing for snow. Chicago as a city, in her opinion, was cleaner than most. But somehow the snow made everything seem clean. The sidewalks. The alleyways. The dingy rooftops. She couldn't wait for winter.

Her strange reaction to Cardic leaving had her on edge. Olivia had too much going on at work to worry about some warped feelings she was having for her fuck buddy. Maybe a few days apart would be best. She could avoid Cardic for at least the first part of the week, but they'd been seeing each other at least every three days for the past two weeks. She either needed to see her less or needed even more control over their encounters. Maybe no more sex at her own place. Having Cardic here, in her space, seemed too personal. Too comfortable.

And comfortable where Cardic was concerned could be dangerous.

❖

"So, what do we notice about warfare with the Yanomami versus warfare with the Yanapo?"

Tyler, a shy, slightly nerdy kid, spoke up. "Well, the Yanomami seem to have a lot more of it."

"And what can we attribute that to? If anything at all?"

"They aren't fighting over females," a jock shouted from the back of the lecture hall, followed by laughs and whistles.

Cardic glanced around at her students, pleased they felt comfortable enough to be themselves but still staying on track with the information. "Well, we know in all sciences, correlation—"

"Does not equal causation," the entire class chanted together.

"Good, pupils. Okay, that's it for today. I've emailed you an article. Be prepared to discuss the social implications of monogamy and polygamy on feminism in sub-Saharan Africa." Cardic waved a dismissive hand at the groans and complaints. "It's two pages, you ungrateful undergrads. See you Wednesday."

After packing up and heading back to her office, Cardic attempted to ignore the pang of disappointment that she had no messages from Olivia. What was there to be disappointed about? The woman had a job. A hard job. With long hours. Cardic was lucky she could get sex from her at all.

"Pat, any messages?" Cardic called through her open door to the outer office as Patrick walked in.

"No, ma'am. But I brought you a coffee."

"I hate when you call me ma'am. But thanks for the coffee."

"I organized the notes from last week. All births and funerals listed by date. Also, chronological list of shaman rituals, color-coded to match those that later died."

In a way, Cardic felt disloyal to the tribe by categorizing, listing, and organizing everything that happened in their lives while she was a part of it all. As if somehow putting it down on paper in order trivialized or devalued the experiences.

"You're amazing. Thanks."

"And Davenport wants to meet with you Thursday. Said it's urgent. Are we getting the ax, Doc?"

"Patrick, are you kidding? You're the best grad assistant in this entire department. Someone will snatch you up if they cut my position. Rest easy."

Patrick looked serious for a moment, then waved a hand and said, "Pish posh. We'll be together forever. Happily ever after."

Why on earth his silly phrase brought Olivia to mind was beyond her, but all the same, Cardic pulled out her cell to text Olivia. Just a quick hello and asked if she wanted to meet for lunch. Funny to think they both worked in the Loop, were less than two miles away from each other all day, and hadn't met for lunch before.

"That's because people that just fuck don't meet for lunch," Cardic whispered to herself.

Cardic was surprised when a few minutes later, she got a

text from Olivia with the address of a corner café where they could meet. They'd seen each other Saturday, but it felt like forever since Cardic had felt her skin, or looked into those bright green eyes.

❖

"A great presentation, Olivia. I'm thrilled. Please keep everything as is with the plus-size line. Don't change a thing."

Olivia felt the breath leave her body in a calming, relieving whoosh. The presentation for Mr. McKinnon had taken her all of Sunday to complete. It wasn't as perfect as she wanted it, like it would have been if she'd worked on it all day Saturday as well, but the day in bed with Cardic gave her a surge of energy and creativity she hadn't expected.

"Thank you, Mr. McKinnon. I've felt very confident about the plus-size line all along, but the most recent focus group gave us some important insights. Thank you so much for taking the time to meet with me." Olivia stood to shake McKinnon's hand and walk him to the elevator, grabbing her purse and sunglasses on the way out.

He reminded her of her father in many ways. He was gentle and calm but still commanding in some way. McKinnon glanced at his watch and gestured for Olivia to precede him out the revolving door into the late-morning sun.

"Are you headed to lunch? May I recommend the Dollop Café? It's actually just around the corner."

The corner of Olivia's mouth lifted, and she remembered her father always said if you find something in common with your boss, you're golden. "I'm actually headed there now. One of my favorite spots."

"I'll walk you. I'm headed down LaSalle for a lunch meeting myself."

"Any particular menu item I should try? I don't think I've had them all yet."

"I'm partial to the BLT."

Knowing that McKinnon was pleased with her work allowed Olivia some measure of respite from the usual ongoing thoughts in her mind. The sidewalk wasn't too crowded, and McKinnon was pleasant company.

As they rounded the corner, Olivia's breath caught. Her steps slowed, and she tried to regain her composure. Seeing Cardic, talking on her cell, sunglasses on, her fingers playing with the dark curls at the nape of her neck, sent a thrill down Olivia's spine.

When Cardic noticed Olivia and her companion approach, she ended her call and walked a few doors down to meet them.

Olivia wasn't sure how to introduce Cardic but knew she was now in a position where she had to. She swallowed. "Mr. McKinnon, this is Dr. Lawson, an acquaintance of mine."

"And your lunch date, I take it from the hungry look on her face. Pleased to meet you, Dr. Lawson."

"Oh, the pleasure's mine. Olivia has only the nicest things to say about you and her experiences at Vital."

"Well, we're the lucky ones. She's really getting things accomplished. The new line is looking great. I'm assuming you'll be joining us for the release party on Friday night?"

Cardic looked at Olivia and smirked, knowing what an awkward situation she'd just put her in. She'd just introduced her booty call to her boss, and he assumed they were an item. Yikes.

"I wouldn't miss it. Olivia can't stop talking about it."

A look of pleased surprise lit McKinnon's face as he walked several steps ahead. "Excellent. Good day then, ladies. Dr. Lawson, see you Friday."

When McKinnon was out of earshot, Olivia punched Cardic on the arm, hard. "Ow! What?"

"What part of sexual, no-strings-attached affair says you come to my work functions?" Olivia looked flustered and annoyed and unbelievably hot.

"What was I supposed to say? 'No, I'm just going to fuck Olivia's brains out after she drinks all your champagne'? He assumed. And I saved you." Many thoughts were running through Cardic's mind at this turn of events, not the least of which was the chance to see Olivia in formal wear.

"I'm screwed."

"What are you worried about? I can schmooze. I'm good-looking, well-spoken, and a doctor. You'll get major points for your taste in women." Cardic dodged the elbow headed for her ribs.

Olivia rubbed her temples as they sat down and waited for their server.

"Olivia, come on. It's just one night. I promise I won't embarrass you. Or we can just call it off."

"No way. I don't want to look like a flake that can't keep a gorgeous, charming doctor for a date."

Cardic's voice dropped, and she rubbed the soft skin on the top of Olivia's hand. "You think I'm gorgeous, huh?"

"In a James Dean meets Indiana Jones kind of way, I suppose." Olivia glanced at the scabbed scrapes and scratches on Cardic's knuckles. She wondered at the power and passion that lay beneath this calm creature in front of her. What did it take to unleash that underlying strength and command of power? Not that Olivia was interested. Cardic was fantastic in the bedroom. She relaxed into Olivia's caress, letting herself be touched and pleased. And in turn, she would please Olivia until she was out of her damn mind.

Their affair had been immensely satisfying thus far, but by always being in control, Olivia was beginning to feel like she was missing out on an entire realm of pleasure where Cardic was concerned.

But the control she wielded seemed to be her only protection. Protection from the new and unwelcome feeling that she and Cardic could be something more. Olivia could not afford to let that control slip.

Chapter Seventeen

The heat of the jungle was sickening, and Cardic tossed and turned on her mat, unable to escape the oppressive blanket of humidity. She glanced around at the still-dark camp and wondered what time it was. Unlike many people, Cardic hadn't been gifted with the ability to sense the time. She needed a clock for anything more specific than day or night.

Cardic stood to stretch her sore muscles, and a light just outside the camp caught her eye. Cardic grabbed her own torch and lit it at the central fire that was always burning. She quietly went toward the light flickering just past the densest trees at the perimeter of the camp.

Bending back heavy branches and vines, Cardic moved toward the light. A group of her tribesmen were standing together surrounding a small fire. At the head of the group were Muap and Tisla, holding hands and gazing into each other's eyes. The eldest shaman stood nearby, speaking in soft tones, trying not to wake the other tribesmen.

"They're getting married," a quiet, female voice said from behind her.

Cardic jumped and was surprised to hear herself yelp. She turned around and was equally shocked to see Olivia standing before her, here in the jungle. "I'm confused. Getting married? But there's—"

"No marriage? Of course there is," Olivia said. "They didn't want you to know. Muap told me you had made up your mind about it and you wouldn't be swayed." Olivia broke into a genuine smile and touched Cardic's arm.

"Olivia, what are you doing here? How did you get here?" Cardic was so dizzy her head began to pound. Cardic grabbed Olivia's hand and leaned against a nearby tree trunk.

"You brought me here. You wanted me to see the place you love so much. The people you love so much." Dirt smeared both of Olivia's cheeks, and her hair looked tangled and unkempt. Her green eyes were bright and alive, and she looked more beautiful than Cardic had ever seen.

A ringing phone brought Cardic back to the present and out of the replay of her dream. It had been so real, she'd woken up in a cold sweat. She'd dreamed of the Yanapo nearly every night since she returned, but this dream troubled her. Not only because of Olivia's presence but because of the strange idea of a secret marriage within the Yanapo tribe. As she grabbed the phone, Cardic hoped it was someone who could distract her from the uneasy memories of the dream.

"Cardic, honey, are you all right? We were so worried when you stormed off on Saturday." Cardic's mom sounded concerned.

Cardic saved the spreadsheet she was working on and prayed for patience. She loved her mother and they had a great relationship, but the one area they never saw eye to eye was her and Claire's permissive attitudes when it came to the fathers of their children. As if the simple act of creating a child entitled these men to a relationship with their children.

"Did you know he was going to be there?" Cardic stretched her still-sore fingers. "It would have saved me some pain if I could have just left before he arrived. Did I upset Claire?"

"Claire was upset with David, not you, dear."

"Did he stay long? Did he cause drama? You know Claire. She's all smiles and hasn't mentioned anything to me."

"She's fine, dear. No, he didn't stay long. Your father stopped by after you left. I wish you could have stayed to see him at least."

Cardic wanted to ask if he'd brought his girlfriend but thought better of it. She didn't want to hurt her mother just to prove a point.

"I was calling to see if you could join Claire and Clark over here tomorrow for dinner."

As much as Cardic loved spending time with her family, it was easy for her to decline when the prospect of spending the evening wining and dining Olivia lay in the future.

"I understand. I like that Olivia."

Cardic rolled her eyes as she packed all her notes in her bag. Patrick left early on Thursdays, and she wanted to get home to walk Cicero.

"Yeah, she's great."

"You could bring her around for the holidays. Your dad told me about his business trip. Too bad you won't have your golf trip with him. I know how much you look forward to that."

A flash of anger hit Cardic like a bat to the head. Her parents had been divorced for nearly a decade, but her father still thought he could keep her mother in the dark about his less-than-noble character.

Instead of dwelling on what she couldn't change, Cardic decided to stop this runaway train in its tracks. "Mom, it's just casual. I doubt I'll even be seeing her by the holidays." The anger she was attempting to tamp down turned suddenly to a strange feeling of loss. Thanksgiving was next month. Was Cardic really saying that she and Olivia were nearing the end of their affair? Who would end it? How would it end?

As she walked to the train, Cardic opened her umbrella

to the light drizzle and whipping wind. She'd had to invest in a quality umbrella, tired of the six-dollar drugstore kind breaking and flipping upside down in the wind.

She and Olivia said their affair would be over when they were both ready to move on. Maybe they wouldn't be ready for a while. What if they could just keep up this system of brief lunches, quick dinners followed by hours in bed? Other than Clark's party and the dinner tomorrow evening, they had stuck to the agreement of casual. What if they could just keep this going as long as they wanted? Why did there have to be a time stamp on it? Maybe things would keep working this way, and they'd still be sleeping together at Christmas.

Cardic jogged the remainder of the block as the rain started to come down harder. Even though her position at Loyola was all but terminated, she felt energized and excited at the thought of continuing to see Olivia for a longer period of time.

Now she just needed to figure out how to pitch the idea to Olivia in a way that wouldn't have her running for the hills.

❖

"How about this one?" Joan held out an off-the-shoulder black cocktail dress with sequins detailing on the neckline.

"No. No black. I have enough black." *And Cardic has already seen me in black. I want to wow her.*

"Why do you even care? I thought you hated these shindigs." Joan made a disgusted face as she pulled another hideous plus-size garment from the rack in the back of the swanky department store. "And you need to go into high fashion. Half these dresses look like potato sacks with glitter."

Olivia sighed and picked up another dress to avoid talking about her interest in an event she'd otherwise detest. "I know. Isn't this sad? Plus-size women always seem to have half a rack of clothes next to the clearance maternity items. We'll get there soon. Tomorrow we do a thorough walkthrough of the first blast of ads, then respond to final preseason purchase orders. I can't believe we're launching in December."

Joan stared at Olivia and walked over to give her a big hug as she wiped a tear from her eye. "I'm so proud of you." Joan leaned behind Olivia and pulled out an emerald green A-line dress with ruching details on the bodice. "This is the one! It matches your eyes perfectly. You'll be sure to pick up a dance partner or two."

Olivia checked the size and price tag. It might be a little on the tight side but was within her budget. The color was rich and the fabric soft and billowy. Her first thought was if Cardic would approve or not. The thought irritated her. She should not be concerned one bit with what Cardic would think about her outfit.

After Olivia tried it on and turned around in front of the mirror a few times, Joan whistled and forbid Olivia to leave the store without it. The fabric draped over her hips and fell in soft waves just above the knee. The bodice was tight but not too tight to be uncomfortable, and her large breasts were encased tightly in the fabric. Like a Victorian debutante! She imagined the look on Cardic's face. Cardic was particularly fond of her breasts.

"I love it."

❖

Cardic pulled at the collar of her starched shirt. Olivia said it wasn't black tie, but not to wear jeans. Cardic settled on black slacks and a white shirt she'd bought for a wedding last year.

Walking up the brick steps of Olivia's apartment building,

Cardic wondered how Olivia would react to the prospect of prolonging their affair. When Olivia opened the door, Cardic forgot everything she was going to say. She forgot who she was and how to breathe.

Olivia's hair was brushed smooth and piled high on top of her head, with gentle wisps of hair brushing her neck. Her eye makeup, darker than usual, sparkled with shades of gray and lavender. Her lips were full and dark in a matte shade that made Cardic ache to kiss her.

After the intense perusal of Olivia's face, Cardic moved her eyes down to her full breasts and long legs. The dark green of the fabric of her dress made her pale skin nearly glow in the evening light.

"Hi," Cardic said, words failing her.

Olivia smiled, obviously pleased with Cardic's speechlessness, "Hi. Let's take a cab. I don't want to be on the train in this dress."

"I don't want you in that dress at all. You look incredible."

Olivia was not prone to blushing, and she had too much makeup on for Cardic to notice if she had been, but she felt heat rise to her cheeks. "You clean up quite well yourself." Olivia rubbed Cardic's arm and clasped her hand as they walked down the sidewalk toward Diversy to catch a cab.

"So how long will this thing take? I was looking forward to seeing you all dressed up, but I have to admit now all I can think of is getting you out of that dress." Cardic ran her hand up Olivia's nape as they rode in the car. She leaned over and whispered, "And I want this hair down spilling over me while you ride me till you come."

Olivia suppressed a moan, feeling herself get wetter by the second. "Will you behave? This is important." If Olivia was this turned on with Cardic by her side just riding in the cab, she'd never be able to focus on work all night. "We have to act normal."

Cardic raised her eyebrows. "What does normal look like?"

Olivia removed Cardic's hand from her knee. "For starters, no touching. No one needs to know the details of our relationship. As far as anyone is concerned, we are very recent acquaintances." Olivia's voice sounded harsher than she'd intended, but she didn't apologize. This was her job. Her livelihood. She wasn't going to let anyone mess it up in any way.

"I see. Should I just stand by the punch bowl all night? Or maybe I could find a good-looking woman to keep my attention."

Olivia tried to ignore the sting of that comment. She worked with many attractive women, some lesbians and some bisexual. And Cardic was the kind of woman who'd make a straight woman question her sexuality. Especially dressed like she was tonight.

"That's fine. Just don't make it seem like we're an item. My personal life is no one's business."

As the Hancock building came into view, Olivia braced herself for an evening she was no longer looking forward to.

❖

Cardic had been admiring Olivia from afar for more than half the evening. When her colleagues started asking how they met and pressing for details about their "relationship," Olivia distanced herself, claiming she needed to talk shop about last-minute details. Cardic knew that was bullshit. As soon as they'd entered the party, McKinnon had come over and greeted them both, congratulating Olivia on a job well done. Done, as in finished.

Now, after some small talk with the cute bartender, Cardic scanned the room for her green-eyed goddess. The fiery red hair stuck out in the crowd, and Cardic found her speaking with a man who'd been introduced to her as Daniel. She was not surprised to see a fond look on Daniel's face as he very obviously glanced at Olivia's breasts as she gestured while she spoke.

"He looks a little too interested in your fox, hon." The bartender slid Cardic another drink.

"I agree," Cardic growled as she headed over to Olivia and her new friend. As she neared, Cardic could tell Olivia was either so enraptured in the conversation that she didn't notice Daniels ogling, or she didn't care.

Sliding her hand around Olivia's waist as she approached, she didn't wait for her to finish speaking before placing a firm kiss on her mouth. Olivia was so surprised that she let out a squeak.

Cardic only intended to peck Olivia's dark lips, but something about the feeling of her nipples brushing against Olivia's arm, and the idea that Daniel could easily see now who would spend the evening kissing Olivia, turned the kiss more heated than she'd intended. Olivia melded into her, and before Olivia opened her mouth to admit Cardic's tongue, Cardic pulled back. "There you are. Thought I'd lost you."

A mixture of arousal and fury swam in Olivia's eyes as Cardic stared down at her, not letting go of her waist.

"Well, here I am," Olivia said in a voice that to anyone else might have sounded singsongy, but to Cardic sounded pissed. And sexy.

"I'm sorry, Daniel, isn't it? I'm afraid I have to steal Olivia for a moment. I'm sure you don't mind."

"Um, no, not at all. Thanks for the information, Liv. I'll be in touch." The man backed away, seeming a little shocked.

"How dare you," Olivia snarled.

"Come with me, *Liv.*" Cardic grabbed Olivia's hand and pulled her toward the long hallway just outside the banquet hall. She found a door marked "Conference Room," tried the knob, and pushed inside.

"What was that, Cardic? I told you to act normal. What the fuck was that?" Olivia wriggled out of Cardic's grasp and walked farther into the room. Other than a small floor lamp in the corner, the room was rather dark. Cardic didn't bother turning on the lights.

"I want to make some amendments to our agreement." Cardic prided herself on being able to stay calm, but when she snapped—she snapped. And right now she felt like a bowstring. One pluck and she'd be done.

"And you had to interrupt a business conversation to discuss it with me?" Cardic could feel the fury rolling off Olivia like heat waves from pavement.

"Business discussion? Are you kidding? The only business on that creep's mind was getting you into bed."

"Daniel?" Olivia's dismissive tone only angered Cardic more.

Cardic stuck both hands in her pants pockets to keep from grabbing at Olivia as she walked closer. Moments ago, the firm press of her jaw had been from anger, but now it seemed to be from a primal need to possess Olivia. To mark her in some way. "Back to my amendment. During this arrangement, I am the only one you will share your body with."

"I don't sleep with men. And I have no idea why you're acting this way." Olivia threw her hands up, the action moving the neckline of her dress down half an inch. "And I thought you didn't believe in monogamy."

"I don't believe in STDs."

Olivia's hand came up to slap Cardic's face so fast she didn't have time to move away. Before Cardic could think about what she was doing, she grabbed the offending hand and pinned it behind Olivia's back.

Olivia's eyes showed no fear, only defiance, and desire. With her mouth close to Cardic's ear, Olivia said, "And what was the other part of our agreement, Dr. Lawson?"

With the sensual tone of Olivia's voice, Cardic felt tempted to forget the suffocating jealousy coursing through her veins. "You're in charge," Cardic growled as she dropped Olivia's hand.

"That's right." Olivia backed up slowly and seemed to take in the room for the first time. The anger from a moment ago seemed to melt away, replaced by an aura of sex and heat and arousal. Cardic felt her clit tighten.

Olivia walked back toward the large conference table and leaned back until her bottom was on the table. With a sweet smile, she moved back with her arms until she was fully sitting on the surface. "So, due to the embarrassment you've caused me, and forgetting the original and most important rule in this agreement, I think you should suffer an appropriate consequence."

Chapter Eighteen

A consequence? And what might that be?"
Olivia gave Cardic a mischievous look and opened her legs just wide enough for Cardic to see the black silk of her panties, then she let the smooth fabric of her dress fall between her legs. "I think you need to come."

"Fine by me." Cardic nearly laughed as she took a step toward Olivia, relieved that she was going to get off before they even left the building. This night had been endless already.

"Not so fast. You're going to come, and since you are so overly concerned with who touches my body, you're going to come here, right now, without touching me at all." Olivia traced the neckline of her dress, pulling at it slightly with her fingertip until Cardic could see the peach of her nipple.

Damn it. "And how the fuck am I supposed to do that?" Cardic stopped a foot away from Olivia's open legs, her hands fisted at her sides.

Olivia took Cardic's hand, put two fingers on her lips, and licked the tips.

Cardic almost exploded. Without permission, Cardic shoved the two fingers into Olivia's mouth. Her tongue and lips were hot and wet, and all Cardic wanted was to rip her clothes off and slide her naked body between Olivia's legs. As she continued to push her fingers in and out of that heavenly mouth, Olivia moaned and pulled away.

"Now, open your pants. Make yourself come."

"Fuck, Olivia. Just let me—"

"No."

Fine. Cardic could play along. Given how hot she was, it would only take a few strokes. Cardic used her other hand to unzip and moved her wet fingers into her boxer briefs. She quickly found a good pace, not even bothering to untuck her shirt.

Olivia's eyes followed the sinewy muscles of Cardic's forearm as she touched herself, her hips jerking slightly, and her eyes never leaving Olivia's.

"Can I please," Cardic said, raising her hand toward Olivia's breast.

Olivia smacked it away, then grabbed the material of her dress and pulled it up her thighs.

Cardic's eyes followed every inch of flesh as it was revealed, her hand a blur now, and her mouth hanging open. God, she was beautiful.

"I'm coming," Cardic panted as she stepped an inch closer to Olivia, resting her fist on the table next to Olivia's thigh.

Olivia took Cardic's face in her hands and kissed her on the lips. Cardic darted her head forward, attempting to deepen the kiss, but Olivia pulled back. "Good girl."

Cardic waited for further instruction. "Now, you're going to make me come." Olivia lifted her hips and slid her panties down, letting them dangle from her left pump. Olivia leaned back on her elbows and gave a contented sound, excited to be delivered from the painful state of arousal she'd been trying to ignore all evening. "You're going to make me come with your mouth only. No hands. Put them behind your back."

Obediently, Cardic dropped to her knees and held her

hands behind her back. Olivia slid her hands into Cardic's dark waves and guided her face between her legs. The moment Cardic's warm tongue met her flesh, Olivia was doomed. She wanted to make it last, she wanted Cardic to lick her and fill her for hours until she couldn't take it anymore. But the way Cardic's tongue pushed and lapped at her, the way she was trying to exhibit control without the use of her hands, Olivia was sure she'd only last a minute.

Olivia thrashed her head and pulled at Cardic's hair, insane with the intense pleasure of controlling Cardic, feeling Cardic's determination to please her at any cost.

Her orgasm started slow and built until she had to bite her hand to keep from calling out as powerful waves of heat rocked her body from head to toe. Olivia squeezed Cardic's head with her thighs, not caring if Cardic could even breathe, just needing to anchor herself to this woman.

Before her body even calmed, Olivia reached for Cardic and kissed her hard, tasting herself on Cardic's lips. In her state of madness, Olivia was angry to feel so many layers of silk and cotton between their bodies. She needed Cardic naked. On top of her. Inside her. Everywhere.

"Take me home."

Sometime later, Cardic glanced at Olivia's alarm clock to find that several hours had passed. Amazing that time away from her crawled, but when they were together seemed to race forward like a bullet. Cardic covered Olivia up to the shoulders with the soft sheet. She propped her head up on her elbow as if intent on staying for a while.

"While I can appreciate your determination, don't look at me like that. No sleepovers."

Cardic hid her disappointment behind a pretend pout as she flopped back on the pillow. "Fine. Then tell me your deepest, darkest secret."

Olivia snorted. "Not a chance." She glanced at Cardic through one eye, seeming intrigued by the topic of secrets. "You tell me a secret. If it's good and juicy, maybe I'll see fit to return one."

Cardic thought for a moment and decided to throw something out. Something she wouldn't tell just anyone. She prayed if she opened up, Olivia would share something with her. Anything to give Cardic a clue about what made her tick. "I'm afraid of being like my father."

After she said it, Cardic realized how true it was and how most things she worked for in life were an attempt to be as unlike him as possible.

Olivia now fully turned to face Cardic and brushed the fiery strands out of her face. Cardic expected her to ask why she didn't want to be like him, but instead, Olivia said, "Tell me how you aren't like him."

"First and foremost is the false promises of monogamy. Dad's big on the illusion of a happy relationship."

Olivia nodded as if she understood even more Cardic's willingness for an unemotional fling.

"And what about your work? Is that a way to set yourself apart as well?"

"I think it started out that way. Dad's not too good with people. I always wondered why. I guess in studying anthropology, I hoped to find the answers to all the questions my father couldn't give me." Cardic hoped this was enough sharing. She started to feel agitated and wanted to talk about Olivia, not her dad.

Olivia arched a brow. "Interesting."

The look on Olivia's face told Cardic she was assessing her in some way. "What?"

"It's interesting to me that, to be as unlike your father as possible, you've made a career out of learning about other cultures, but have trouble finding intimacy in your own life."

Cardic bristled at the assessment. Why did she even bring this up? There was plenty of intimacy in her life. Her mother, Claire and Clark, Patrick. The more she replayed Olivia's words in her mind, the more uneasy she became.

Olivia shifted on the bed, realizing she might have hit a nerve. She took stock of Cardic's posture and looked for any signs she was about to get out of the bed and leave. "I didn't mean..." Olivia didn't know what she didn't mean, only that she hadn't meant to offend Cardic.

Cardic didn't respond; she only reached for her phone from the bedside table. The screen lit up as she checked the display.

Afraid she would leave any moment but not ready for her to go, Olivia reached over and rubbed Cardic's arm.

"I don't remember my mother."

Cardic put her phone down and put her full attention on Olivia. "I thought you said she left when you were eight?"

Olivia fought the sick feeling in her stomach but pushed forward. Maybe it would help her to get it out. She never talked about her mother. Not even with her dad.

"That's the weird part. I have a great memory. I can remember the shirt I wore on the first day of kindergarten. It was pink with a white cat on it. But my mother...I've pushed those memories so far away that I can't even reach them anymore."

Cardic gave an understanding smile and laced her fingers with Olivia's. "I think we all try to forget things that upset us. Like punching former brothers-in-law at birthday parties." As her full smile appeared, Cardic bent over and kissed Olivia on the mouth.

Olivia was grateful for the small joke to ease the moment and prayed she would be able to remember every moment with Cardic when their affair was over.

❖

Monday morning came too quickly for Cardic. They'd spent Friday night in Olivia's bed, and much to Cardic's disappointment, and despite their intimate talk of fears and memories, she'd been given the boot around dawn on Saturday morning. She could and would continue to respect Olivia's request for no sleepovers, but even if Cardic had stayed, there would have been no sleep.

The last time Cardic had sex like this was in college. And even that paled in comparison. In college, her sexual experiences usually involved alcohol, curiosity, and fumbling around in an extra-long twin bed. And Cardic had never slept with someone with this level of stamina. She could get Olivia off, and before she'd even caught her breath, Olivia would be ready again. It was addictive.

Cardic still needed to broach the subject of prolonging their affair into the new year. The sex was doing her good. She had more energy, she was hyperfocused at work, and she'd been able to keep up with Clark on their play dates. Olivia was a sexy fountain of youth. But something in the back of her mind told her Olivia would want to be done with things sooner rather than later. Even though they had been sticking to the no-strings rule, the no-sleepovers rule, the Olivia's-in-charge rule, something seemed to be changing in their dynamic. Especially after their tryst on Friday in the conference room at the Hancock building and their pillow talk later. Cardic couldn't put her finger on it, but she liked it very much. And her gut told her Olivia wouldn't.

❖

Patrick dropped a FedEx receipt on Cardic's desk and walked over to the small table in the back of Cardic's office where he'd been grading a stack of Intro to Anthropology papers. If her position was cut next semester, she would miss these breaks in between classes, when she and Patrick would pore over student work, even if the ungraded stack of papers never seemed to get any smaller. "Say, Dr. Lawson?"

Cardic knew she wasn't going to like this. Patrick never called her Dr. Lawson. "What's up?"

"I couldn't help but notice that adorable little package addressed to Ms. Reynolds. Just curious if anything in the box could possibly pertain to a hot, sweaty fling?"

Cardic cringed. She'd hoped Patrick wouldn't notice the small box buried in the bag of outgoing mail.

On her way home the night before, Cardic had met a hippie woman on the sidewalk selling homemade jewelry. The green geode had caught Cardic's attention immediately. It matched Olivia's eyes perfectly. "Well, I'll have you know there are some items that could fit in that box that could pertain to a hot, sweaty fling. And I'll just let you wonder about it for a while."

"The miracle of lesbian sex does not interest me in the slightest."

Cardic decided to turn the tables and walked over to Patrick to return the phrase. "Say, Mr. Brown?"

"What's up, Doc? Hey, why ya getting so close?" Patrick shrieked and moved away from Cardic, pulling the collar of his lavender button-down a little farther up his neck.

Cardic pointed to the very obvious purple bruise on Patrick's neck. "The new boy's handiwork?" Cardic laughed.

"Hey. It's not my fault, he was enthusiastic."

"Just try to keep it covered. Maybe wear a paper bag over your head tomorrow." Cardic dodged a flying paper clip as she reached for the ringing phone.

"Lawson." Cardic's smile dropped when she heard the voice on the other end of the line.

"Cardic. It's Megan. It's been a long time."

A long time, but her sultry voice sounded just the same. "Megan, hi. I got your message the other week. I just haven't had a chance to call you back. I'm kind of swamped." *And I've been spending almost every free moment naked with Olivia.*

"Yes, your ethnography. I can imagine. Congratulations on landing a publishing deal."

"Thank you. Yes, I was very fortunate. I'm sure anthropologists will be all over the Yanapo soon."

"Indeed. Listen, that's actually why I'm calling. My sabbatical from Brown was approved, and I'll be completing a field study of my own on a tribe neighboring the Yanapo. They are located about fifty kilometers from the original group you stayed with."

"Megan, that's great. Congratulations to you."

"Well, hopefully, congratulations to us. I want you to come with me. I really don't have a grasp of the language yet, and I'd benefit from your expertise."

Cardic's heart clenched, and she pulled out her chair to sit. Cardic took a deep breath, ran a hand through her hair, and attempted to sound normal. "Wow, Megan. I'm honored. When do you leave?" Cardic asked more out of manners and curiosity than actual interest. There was no way she could leave her family again. Or Olivia. Or her job. Her job that was in jeopardy. But being with her tribe again? The people. The plants and animals. The quiet away from the city. It was tempting, to say the least.

"I'm finalizing budgeting plans with my investors, but

hoping to leave at the end of the spring semester. Are you interested? We could meet to discuss it? Maybe over dinner?"

"You know what, let me check my calendar and get back to you." Other than all the pleasant side effects of her affair with Olivia, Cardic had become rather flaky. Always holding off on plans to wait and see if she'd be able to see Olivia.

"Sure." Megan's voice dropped slightly and took on a rather sexual tone. "We were great partners in college. I'd love to make this work."

Unlike most times when Cardic was the object of someone's flirting, this time her skin crawled. Cardic didn't want to hear a voice like that from anyone but Olivia.

After disconnecting with Megan, Cardic swiveled around in her chair to look at her home away from home. The minute she left the Amazon, she knew she would jump at the chance to return. But now the chance was staring her in the face, and the only thing she could think about was Olivia.

❖

Going back and forth between being turned on and appalled by Cardic's display of irrational jealousy was irritating and confusing to Olivia. She and Cardic had both agreed to this no-strings affair, and so far, with minor exceptions, they'd both stuck to their guns. But something about the possessive fire in Cardic's eyes, the firm set of her jaw, and the image of Cardic becoming physically aggressive on her behalf was... sexy. That wasn't something Olivia had ever expected or even wanted from a lover.

"Mail's here," Vivian sang as she breezed through the door.

"You're in a good mood." Olivia shook her head. Vivian had really blossomed over the last few weeks. She shared more of her ideas, she fought back when she disagreed with Olivia, and she was working harder than ever. "Vivian, come take a seat for a moment." *Credit where credit is due.*

Vivian looked nervous for a moment, then straightened her spine and sat in one of the chairs flanking Olivia's desk, "Ma'am?" Vivian smirked at Olivia, knowing she hated being called ma'am.

"I just wanted to thank you for your amazing work the last few weeks. I don't always like being challenged by others, as you can imagine, but you've brought some important ideas to the table, and I thank you for not holding back. You were an important part of this Vital project."

"Well, no, thank you, Olivia. Seriously. You've been like a different person. I knew you'd have high expectations for this relaunch campaign, but you've just been so…I don't know… approachable."

Olivia wasn't quite sure how to respond to that praise. Was she losing her touch? She'd always believed women in the workplace needed to be hard and unbending. As she continued to examine her own behavior and work relationships, she realized Melissa had even begun to show more civility toward her, even stopping by her office to say good morning most days. Still unsure what to say, Olivia just blurted, "Thank you."

"Anyway, here's your mail. You got a cute package! Is that from your dad?" Vivian handed over a stack of papers and a small box wrapped in brown butcher paper. There was no return address.

Olivia put aside the other letters and pulled open the small package. She opened the lid of the box and found a small emerald-colored geode hanging from a delicate gold chain. The jewel sparkled with shades of green, gold, and jade. The detail was incredible. It was breathtaking.

Vivian gasped. "God, that's gorgeous!"

Olivia lifted the card from below the trinket and saw what she assumed was Cardic's handwriting. She'd never seen her handwriting before. It was neat and slanted slightly; she knew Cardic was left-handed. Somehow reading her handwriting seemed more intimate to Olivia than receiving a beautiful piece of jewelry.

The small card read, *Thanks for a fantastic weekend. I saw this and thought of your eyes—Cardic.*

At least she didn't sign it *Love, Cardic.* There was no room for love in this arrangement. There was only room for sex. Olivia squeezed her thighs together in an attempt to feel anything other than the girlish glee she couldn't seem to suppress. When she was a little girl, before her mother left, she'd often thought about meeting someone who would send her flowers and candy and jewelry. Someone she'd marry someday. But that's not how she wanted it now. That's not how she had very carefully planned her career and life to turn out.

Yes, now she was angry. A much safer emotion. "I gotta go. I'll be back in an hour."

Chapter Nineteen

The longer the morning dragged on, the more apprehensive Cardic became about sending a gift to Olivia. Cardic knew it was due to arrive at her office today, and she wondered if she should have just waited and given it to her in person.

When the door to the outer office opened, Cardic assumed Patrick was back from his lunch break until she heard the sound of expensive heels clacking against the tile.

"Why did you send this to my office?" Olivia barged into Cardic's office without knocking, holding out the offending item.

"Hello to you, too." Cardic grinned at Olivia. She had a hunch this might be her reaction.

"Tell me why. Now my entire office will be asking me when you're going to propose and where we will honeymoon!"

Cardic had to mentally shake herself from the image of her and Olivia making love on a secluded beach somewhere. A honeymoon didn't sound too bad. Cardic knew she was smiling and she didn't care, which only seemed to fuel Olivia's anger.

"I'm serious, Cardic."

Cardic stood and walked around her desk toward Olivia. "What? I can't send you a small token of my appreciation for a fabulous time in bed?"

"No!"

Cardic couldn't put her finger on it, but she was growing irritated that Olivia couldn't just take the gift. Not only that, but why she so wholeheartedly objected to it. Locking angry gazes with Olivia, Cardic stalked closer. "And why not?" Cardic asked louder, her voice now matching the level of Olivia's.

"Because we aren't dating, we're fucking!"

In an instant Olivia was on her, attacking her mouth. Running her hands through her hair, pulling at her clothes. Cardic broke away first, Olivia still groping at her and pushing her crotch into Cardic's, begging for more contact.

All of Cardic's anger clashed with her teetering control and she snapped. Grabbing Olivia by the arms, she spun her around and walked her toward her large desk. "So you want me to fuck you?" In the spirit of their affair thus far, Cardic decided to still ask permission before going full force and taking what she wanted. Needed. As she palmed Olivia's ass and rubbed her breasts, Cardic repeated her question in a harsh whisper.

Olivia mumbled her reply. "I can't hear you." Cardic grabbed Olivia's breasts with both hands and rocked her pelvis into Olivia's ass.

"Yes."

"Then ask. Nicely," Cardic growled as she pushed Olivia the rest of the way toward her desk until the tops of her thighs met the solid oak.

"Please," Olivia whispered.

Cardic ran her hand up Olivia's back, reaching the collar of her shirt and guiding the top half of her body to rest on the desk. Olivia rested her large breasts on top of the files and papers all over the desk as Cardic reached the hem of her skirt. Cardic slid her hand up the inside of Olivia's thigh, and she seemed to almost unconsciously open her legs wider to allow Cardic admittance.

When Cardic saw Olivia barge into her office, this was not what she had planned. She hadn't expected to be bitched at for sending a gift. But the minute she saw the angry look in Olivia's eyes, she was turned on. She wanted her. She wanted to make her come. In her office. On her desk. In her mouth. And she wasn't going to wait to be told what to do.

Her hands shook as she continued to smooth her hands over Olivia's thighs and backside. Part of the reason she wanted to take Olivia from behind was to hide her own need and desperation. Up until this point, the power dynamic was somewhat of an illusion to Cardic. She had no trouble admitting to being turned on and needing to come, but exposing the fact that she needed Olivia's body more than she needed her next breath made her feel too raw and vulnerable.

Cardic pushed the thoughts from her mind and concentrated on the fact that she had this beautiful, fiercely sexual creature writhing with need beneath her fingers.

"I don't think you mean that." Cardic tugged at Olivia's hair and bent to lick the shell of her ear. "You didn't come here because you're angry. You came here for me to fuck you." Cardic moved her hand to Olivia's panties and probed her opening through the thin fabric. "And I'm not going to, until you admit that." Cardic was having trouble stringing together sentences.

"Yes."

"Yes, what?"

"Yes, I came here for you…for you to…"

Cardic tugged on her hair and slipped the flimsy panties down Olivia's thighs, just waiting for her to finish her admission.

"…to fuck me."

With that, Cardic entered her and began a rough, slow massage with her fingers. Olivia groaned and pumped her ass into Cardic's hand. The feeling of being filled by Cardic was unlike anything she'd ever experienced, but she needed more. Olivia reached down with her left hand, intending to stroke her clit as Cardic continued to pump in and out of her. But Cardic had other ideas.

"Grab the far edge of the desk. Hold on to it." Cardic's voice was controlled and even, but Olivia could feel the desire coursing through her anywhere their skin touched. For the first time she could recall, Olivia obeyed another human being during a sexual encounter. She reached far in front of her and grabbed the edge of the desk; the action stretched her arms uncomfortably but deepened the feeling of Cardic's fingers.

Olivia bit her lip, on the brink of screaming as she rose to the peak and Cardic rushed to push her over, rubbing her hips against her own hand and Olivia's ass. Olivia exploded. Every atom of her body vibrated. Her body trembled and her breath hitched. Olivia took in a rush of air as her body lay limp on the desk.

Tears pricked Olivia's eyes, and she lay facedown on Cardic's desk, trying to make sense of what just happened. She moaned as Cardic continued to milk every last tremor and sensation from her body. Olivia felt too vulnerable and open to turn around. She wanted to run. Out of this office and away from this woman. But something inside her pushed her to stand up and look at Cardic's face. Olivia pushed herself to a standing position and hesitated before turning around.

Cardic stood before her, looking like a statue of Greek mythology. Her eyes wide and dark, her jaw clenched, all her muscles tensed and bunched. Sweat ran down her temples. Something in Olivia changed. She no longer wanted to tell Cardic what to do. She no longer wanted to control every touch and caress. She wanted to make Cardic come. Any way she wanted.

Olivia grabbed Cardic's face with both hands and kissed her, slowly. As if kissing her for the first time, Olivia's attention was drawn to the smoothness of Cardic's lips, the firm press of her jaw. The scent of her breath. She brushed the damp strands of hair from Cardic's brow. "Tell me what you need."

Cardic closed her eyes and continued taking deep breaths, her voice hoarse with desire. "Make me come."

Olivia smiled. Cardic always asked permission to orgasm. But she seemed to be missing the point. Olivia didn't just want to make her come. She wanted Cardic to tell her what to do. To demand it of her. To control her.

"Tell me what to do."

Cardic's eyes snapped open, and she focused on Olivia through a haze of lust. Seeming to understand, Cardic grabbed Olivia's wrist and moved it to her pants. "Start with your fingers. Finish with your mouth."

Olivia knelt in front of Cardic and unbuckled her belt and pants. This was a first for Olivia. She'd often been in the reverse position, but never had she knelt in front of a woman to follow her commands. It was new and it was okay because it was Cardic. Olivia moaned at the realization that she was completely giving over her power.

Olivia used two fingers to rub and tease Cardic's flesh as she waited for instruction. Olivia was used to doing what she wanted, taking what she wanted. But right now, all she wanted was for Cardic to command her every movement. Freedom from control, freedom from planning, and freedom from thinking filled Olivia with a sexual joy. It was similar to the most gratifying success she'd experienced in her career, only she didn't have to work for it.

No decisions, only compliance.

"Harder." Cardic fisted a handful of Olivia's hair and guided her mouth forward. "Now your tongue, but go slow." Her voice was tight and gruff.

Olivia used her tongue and fingers as instructed. She closed her eyes as her body sang with the satisfaction of pleasing Cardic. For Olivia, getting a woman off was usually just a precursor to her own orgasm. Never had she given thought ahead to the pleasure she could provide her partner, to the connection she could create.

Cardic came with a groan as the full extent of Olivia's thoughts dawned on her. Connecting to another person? She was confused. Something new was happening. That wasn't part of the deal. This was just sex. No strings. No expectations. And absolutely no connection.

As Cardic righted herself and ran her hands through her hair, Olivia studied her face. Beautiful. *What are you thinking? And why do I care?* Dangerous territory.

"Olivia, that was…" Cardic said, a strained look on her face. She'd broken Olivia's one rule. And Olivia had let her.

"Yes, it was."

"Listen, if I…"

"No. You didn't do anything wrong." That was a complete surprise. Now after the very unsettling feeling of emotion moments before, she was now even more concerned with Cardic's reaction. Olivia glanced at her watch and realized how much time had passed. She gave Cardic a weak smile as she straightened her skirt and blouse. "I'm not running, but I really do have to go."

When Cardic only nodded, Olivia stepped past her toward the door. Her throat tightened as Cardic grabbed her wrist and rubbed her knuckles. Olivia didn't turn around.

"When can I see you?"

"I'll call you." And without looking back, Olivia walked out.

❖

"Megan called me."

"Megan, the she-devil?"

Cardic rolled her eyes at her sister's dramatic choice of words. Her relationship with Megan had indeed been intense and at times volatile, but she wouldn't refer to her as the devil. Claire glared at Cardic, waiting for more details as she stirred honey into her tea. Cardic was always amazed her sister could drink hot tea year-round, even in the Chicago summer heat.

"She's heading to Brazil for her own field study of a neighboring Yanapo tribe."

"Good for her," Claire said dismissively, studying her fingernails.

"She wants me to go with her."

Now Cardic had Claire's full attention. Cardic looked at her with a mix of excitement and absolute dread. "I know how much you loved it there. But you just got back."

"I'm not going."

Claire blew out a breath and tossed a balled-up napkin at Cardic, "Then why tell me at all?"

"I couldn't leave you and Clark. And this is such a special time in his little life. I don't want to miss another second of it."

"Well, I don't want you to jeopardize an important opportunity, but I will be completely selfish and tell you again that I don't want you to go."

Cardic knew it took a lot for Claire to admit that. Claire only wanted others to be happy, even at her own expense. Claire's reaction only cemented in her mind that she was making the right decision.

"I don't want to leave you and Clark. But there's more." Cardic avoided her curious stare and braced herself for whatever reaction might follow.

"Okay?"

"Of course I don't want to leave you and Clark, but I don't...I'm not ready to leave Olivia. I didn't even realize it until Megan called. But after you guys, she's the only other person I don't want to be without."

"Wow. That is surprising. I mean, don't get me wrong. She seems wonderful, but I thought your relationship was *not* a relationship?"

"I guess that's the problem. It's not. A relationship. And I'm not saying that's what I want. But I know whatever we have, I'm not ready for it to end."

"And how does she feel?"

Cardic pictured Olivia on her knees waiting to be commanded. Cardic knew Olivia well enough to know that was new for her, and she would have to process what that encounter had meant to her. But Cardic knew what it meant for herself. Seeing Olivia, vulnerable, subordinate, open, and responsive, Cardic wanted her that way again. And often. "I have a feeling she senses the dynamic changing between us, and she is getting nervous."

"Changing how?"

Slightly uncomfortable at discussing the particulars of a sexual affair with her own sister, Cardic hesitated and tried to find a way to explain. "She wants things a certain way. To keep me at a distance. Which I thought I was okay with. But now... Now I want to get inside her head. I want to know what she's thinking. And I don't know how she feels about it."

"You can't just talk to her about it?"

"If only it were that easy. I don't want to scare her off."

"Does she know Megan called?"

"No. Well, actually yes. She knows Megan called and left me a message. But that wouldn't bother her. She's very confident in herself and doesn't get jealous."

"No, no, not because you're exes. Does she know there's a chance you could be leaving again?"

"I'm not leaving."

"Right, but she doesn't know that. You could bring it up just to see how she responds. Since you don't feel like you can discuss it with her honestly and openly, maybe you could just test the waters?"

Cardic thought for a moment. Her sister's choice of words felt like a jab. Couldn't she be honest and open with Olivia? Couldn't she just ask how Olivia felt about what was going on between them? In a word—no. Olivia's need for control, order, and predictability outweighed her ability to have an honest conversation about something that could threaten her perfectly organized existence.

Chapter Twenty

S o, explain it to me again."

Olivia glared at Joan from across the couch. She had planned to get some work done at the office today; Saturdays were usually so quiet, and she could get tons of work done by herself with no interruptions. But this morning, after she'd been tortured all night by dreams of Cardic, Olivia couldn't bring herself to get out of bed and get dressed.

Joan had first called her office to get in touch with her, as she usually did on Saturday mornings. When there was no answer, Joan rushed over to see if Olivia was okay. That was about two hours ago. Now here they sat on Olivia's couch after she spilled her guts about everything that happened with Cardic. Her love for the Yanapo. The jealous episode at her work party. Olivia giving up control. It all came pouring out.

"I already explained it to you. Things changed when we slept together in her office. I'm not comfortable with it. I think it's time to end things."

"But wait. Let's just look at the facts. You like sleeping with her?"

Olivia resisted the urge to moan and squeezed her thighs together. "Yes, very much."

Joan sipped the homemade lemonade Olivia had made yesterday. When something personal was bothering her, which was rare, she'd often spend time in the kitchen trying to avoid thinking about it.

"You also like her as a person?"

"We constantly bicker and irritate each other, but overall I'd say yes."

"Everything was going fine until you let her top you in her office?"

"Yes, I suppose."

"Easy fix. Just tell her you want things back the way they were. Then you can keep sleeping with her, and you won't be this weirdo June Cleaver who makes homemade lemonade and quiche."

"You said the quiche was amazing."

"It was, but you must be really stressed if you're attempting French cuisine."

It's funny that cooking seemed to be one of the things Olivia did to relieve stress. Her mother loved to cook, and Olivia was always in the kitchen with her. Olivia thought it strange that something that caused her so much pain—memories of her mother—would have somehow morphed into a coping mechanism.

❖

Cardic ran her hands through her hair as she attempted to concentrate on the term papers in front of her. The students in her two-hundred-level class had learned a lot and were expressing their ideas well, but Cardic couldn't bring herself to be enthusiastic at the moment. She thought of Olivia as she ran her hands over the smooth wood of her desk, bent over and moaning her name.

Olivia called as she promised the following day, but they

had not gotten together again. Cardic felt sure Olivia was still dealing with what happened.

Cardic looked at the clock and thought about calling Olivia and demanding that they get together. But perhaps her requests were the problem. Olivia was freaking out because Cardic had demanded things of her. Cardic had changed their game and she was suffering the consequences.

"Hey, Doc?" Patrick broke Cardic's fragile concentration. It wasn't like she was getting much done anyway.

Cardic closed the folder of mostly ungraded papers and pushed back in her chair. "What's up, Patrick?"

"Does Yako have a sister?"

With some members of the tribe, especially the ones she hadn't gotten to know well, Cardic would have needed to look at her notes, but she'd spent so much time with Yako, she knew immediately he did not have a sister. He was the youngest of four brothers.

Cardic dropped her hands in exasperation, "No. No sister. Why do you ask?"

Patrick was busy organizing the duplicates of any pictures Cardic had taken and sorting them by yano and individual tribesman for easy reference. "Then who's this woman he is always with? I haven't gotten to his picture but noticed she doesn't live in yano number four with him."

Cardic furrowed her brows and walked toward Patrick. She knew Yako lived in a yano with two of his brothers, and his mother and eldest brother lived in yano number two, not far away.

"Which woman?" Patrick handed a group of photographs to Cardic and pointed at the young woman's face in several of them. Nalya. In all the pictures, she and Yako were next to each other or in the same group of tribesmen. In one picture, they were cooking a traditional Yanapo stew. In another, Yako was swinging in a hammock as Nalya attended to several children on the floor of the yano. Cardic glanced at the wall display to search the images, notes, and timelines for the picture she was thinking of.

"Here they are again." Cardic pointed to the picture taken during the birth of Nalya's first child, Sanya.

"Oh yeah." Patrick ran over to the box of photos that he'd already finished organizing, "That's Sanya. I already got to his photos. The kid has the best eyes."

Cardic's head snapped up and she grabbed the photos of the baby. She held one up to a picture of Yako's intense golden eyes. "Bingo."

"I think you mean D-A-D. But what does all this mean?"

"Okay, so if Yako fathered Sanya, and he spends most of his leisure time and special occasions with Nalya, I'd venture to guess there is a level of commitment here."

"I thought this tribe is non-monogamous? They don't even have a marriage ceremony?"

"You're right, and they don't." Cardic again searched all the pictures and faces. She tacked the pictures of the young boy underneath pictures of who Cardic assumed to be his father. Cardic needed to think about this logically. Just because Yako fathered Nalya's child didn't mean they had a monogamous relationship. Just because he was present for Sanya's birth, and attended every ceremony she had photographed with or near Nalya, didn't mean he wasn't sleeping with other tribeswomen.

But maybe he doesn't want to.

An image of Olivia flashed in Cardic's mind. Her fiery red hair, bright green eyes. That genuine smile she tried so hard to hide. Her drive and passion for work. And for sex. Cardic imagined coming home to Olivia every night. Sleeping in on the weekends and bringing her breakfast in bed. She imagined all the things she'd once mocked people for wanting, and realized with a punch to the gut that she wanted those things.

If Cardic never slept with another waitress or flight attendant again, she'd be fine as long as she could come home to someone special.

"Doc, you all right? You're looking a little pale. Why don't you sit down?"

"Patrick. I think..." Cardic wiped her face with both hands, trying to slow the racing thoughts in her head. "I think I have a problem."

"Hey, come on. So there's one bad apple. Just 'cause he has a woman, it doesn't throw your theory to the wind." Patrick pulled out several pictures from the photo box. "Like check out this guy, he's always gettin' his." Patrick did a little jig as he pointed out one of the more eligible tribesmen, Sekya.

"No, no. It's Olivia. I think, I..." Cardic hesitated searching for the words she knew she needed to utter aloud but not knowing if she could. Once she let them out, it would be like floods from a dam. There'd be no taking it back.

"Oh, you love her. Yeah, I know." Patrick cocked his head to the side and stared at Cardic like she'd just told him the sky was blue or fish swam.

"But how did you know? I didn't even know. And how can I be sure?"

"First, you haven't been staring at Dr. Coleman's ass every time she leaves the room." Stephanie Coleman had the office next door and often stopped by to borrow staples or Post-its. Long ago, Cardic entertained the idea of sleeping with her but thought better of it. Cardic had never slept with a colleague. Stephanie did have a great ass, but lately, Cardic really hadn't thought much about it.

"Next, every time the phone rings I can hear the disappointment in your voice when it's not Olivia."

This one Cardic couldn't really argue with. It was true. Up until a moment ago, she would have said the prospect of awesome sex was the only motivator behind wanting to hear Olivia's voice on the line. But now it seemed appropriate to say she just wanted to talk. To ask how her day was going.

"And the last one is a little hokey but totally true." Patrick sat next to Cardic and placed a hand on her arm. "You've just been really happy. With a hop in your step. You've always been laid back, but truth be told, there was something somber and lonely about you. I kinda thought it was part of your personality. But now I see Olivia really brings out the best in you."

Cardic attempted a smile, but it turned into more of a grimace. How could she have turned into one of those people? One of those lovesick fools who only a few months ago she thought were full of shit? Everything she'd worked hard to prove about herself fell apart the moment she admitted she held any emotion stronger than lust. What about everything she'd ever told Claire? Love was a manufactured emotion designed to sell greeting cards. Something people convinced themselves they felt to validate their own existence. What about all that?

"Are you going to tell her?"

Cardic imagined the look on Olivia's face if the L-word were to come out of her mouth. It'd probably be similar to the look of fear in her eyes when Cardic had initially proposed their no-strings-attached fling. Similar to the alarm on her face when Cardic tried to stake her claim on Olivia at the celebration party. It would also probably resemble the face Olivia made, right here in this office, as she surrendered all control and let Cardic take what she wanted. A face filled with desire and longing. And rampant with fear. Olivia was already scared out of her wits and prepared to run at any second. Why not throw her feelings at her, all of them, everything at once and see where things went?

"Hell yes, I'm going to tell her." Cardic stood and grabbed her bag, looking back at Patrick, who'd gone back to organizing photos. "Hey, Pat, thanks."

"Go get 'em, Tiger." Patrick waved a hand as if it were just another day. Just another day when Cardic threw out all her convictions and surrendered to the one thing in life she thought was good for no one. Love.

❖

Olivia set the oven to preheat, then used a rubber pastry brush to add an egg wash to the homemade piecrust. After mulling over her conversation with Joan, Olivia made the decision to give Cardic two options. Either they returned to the original rules of their arrangement or they ended things now. Either of which was fine with Olivia. If Cardic didn't agree and wanted to end things, so be it. Olivia could find another fuck buddy. She did have to admit the amazing sex had done wonders for her concentration at work and apparently, according to Vivian, was making her more pleasant to be around. And if Cardic agreed to continue their affair under the predetermined rules, then great. Olivia had to admit there was something sexy about the way Cardic grabbed her hand and demanded her touch. The way she tried to keep her tense muscles still as she whispered her commands. But it wasn't what Olivia wanted. She wanted to be in control, like before. She wanted to call the shots.

And as evident by the apple pie in the making, Olivia felt totally confident in her decision to give Cardic an ultimatum.

As she checked the time, Olivia repeated the mantra she'd had since college: *Sleep is for the weak.* It was already close to nine, and the pie would need to cook for close to an hour. All this feeling and deciding wore on Olivia's nerves. What she really wanted to do was crawl under her down comforter and go to sleep. A knock at the door pulled her from her work in the kitchen. She hadn't buzzed anyone in, so it must be Mrs. Harper from downstairs. Sometimes she stopped by to borrow an egg or toilet paper.

Olivia continued to read the directions on her recipe card as she opened the door. The card slipped from her fingers as soon as Cardic's chocolate brown eyes greeted her.

"Cardic. Hi."

"Hi. Sorry, someone was leaving downstairs, so I just stepped in." Cardic glanced behind Olivia then at her floral print apron, a small smile tugging at her full lips "Is this a bad time?"

"No. I was just…" Olivia picked up the recipe card and hesitated. She didn't share her stress-relief cooking with many people, but Cardic had caught her in the act. "I was just making a pie. For my dad. He likes apple pie. Especially in the fall." Now she was rambling.

As Olivia moved back to allow Cardic entrance, Cardic remembered not long ago she had wished that she could see Olivia without makeup. Her makeup was always flawless and natural looking, but as Cardic stared down at Olivia in the doorway of her apartment, a faint smattering of freckles on her nose and smudges of flour on both cheeks, Cardic realized she'd never in her life seen anyone so beautiful. Cardic licked her finger and moved forward to wipe away some of the flour left from Olivia's pie making. "You've got a little…"

The intimacy of the movement struck a chord inside

Cardic. As she brushed her thumb over Olivia's skin, she felt like she was seeing her, and touching her for the first time. Cardic knew there were things she needed to say, there were things they both needed to own up to, agree upon. But a subtle force inside was guiding her in a completely different direction.

Cardic cupped the back of Olivia's head and moved forward until their bodies were flush. She wasn't asking for permission, and she wasn't waiting to be commanded or directed. As Olivia's hands came up to her shoulders, her eyes softened, and she bit her bottom lip. Cardic could see the struggle on her face. No doubt Olivia had things she needed to say as well.

But neither of them spoke. Their bodies brushed and touched as if becoming acquainted for the first time. An inch at a time, Cardic lowered her mouth to Olivia's, waiting for Olivia to stop her, to take control, to do something. But she didn't. Olivia closed her eyes and sank into Cardic's touch, sighing as if being in Cardic's embrace was the only place she'd ever wanted to be. Imagining that was how Olivia felt made Cardic feel ten feet tall, even though chances were high Olivia was too frightened of what was going on between them to admit to anything. Or feel anything. Cardic continued to press her tongue into Olivia's mouth, nipping at her lips. Maybe if Cardic could turn her on enough, please her enough, Olivia would confess her love as well, and everything wouldn't turn to shit.

Overcome with the emotion and reality of this moment, and what it meant for her life and everything she'd ever believed in, Cardic felt weak in the knees. She felt overcome with a sense of connection and rightness. The feeling was so strong she hoped she wouldn't blurt out something stupid.

Instead of sinking her teeth into Olivia's skin, she would need to bite her own tongue. If only they could stay locked in this moment—Cardic completely in love and Olivia completely oblivious. But it wasn't enough for Cardic. It wouldn't be enough. She rested her forehead against Olivia's and said the only thing she thought Olivia might respond positively to. "Take me to bed."

CHAPTER TWENTY-ONE

As she took Cardic's hand and led her to the dark bedroom, Olivia felt her skin prickle at the tension and vulnerability radiating off Cardic's body. Had something happened at work? Cardic had mentioned her teaching position being in jeopardy, but Olivia hadn't wanted to pry. They were only lovers, after all, not partners in a relationship. Whatever was going on had put Cardic in a state of need like Olivia had never seen. It was foreign and intense. The look in those brown eyes crept into a place Olivia could only describe as her heart.

Somehow, the typical protocol of their affair seemed cheap and unfeeling. Cardic needed support, and the only support Olivia was capable of offering was that of her body. Instead of telling Cardic how or where to undress, instead of telling her to get on the bed or kneel on the floor, Olivia guided her to the bed and pushed on her shoulders gently until she sat on the edge of the bed. Olivia took a step back, but not out of reach. She shuddered as she undressed and Cardic caressed the areas of skin she revealed.

When she stood naked in front of Cardic, Olivia was surprised to find Cardic's arms come around her middle in a sweet embrace as she smoothed her lips over the skin of Olivia's stomach. So far Olivia had been able to keep her apprehension at bay, but something about the intimacy of those strong arms around her and the lack of lust accompanied by them seemed too much. Removing Cardic's hands from her body, she walked around the bed and pulled the sheets down. Anything to get away from Cardic's intoxicating vulnerability.

Cardic stood, undressing mechanically, laying her clothes over an accent chair as if she slept in Olivia's room every night. Olivia quivered as she watched the smooth planes of Cardic's stomach bunch and then relax as she removed her shirt. The muscles and veins in Cardic's arms strained as she unbuckled her belt and shoved her pants and boxers down.

Rubbing her tattoo, Cardic walked naked to the bed and crawled in the other side.

Despite the alarm bells going off in her head, Olivia pulled Cardic toward her until they tangled together in a heap of limbs, kissing and touching. They'd slept together in as many places and ways as Olivia could count, but this felt like the first time Olivia had ever touched Cardic. It felt like the first time she'd ever touched anyone.

After what felt like minutes but could have been hours, Olivia couldn't take the burn any longer. "Cardic, please, I need you." It was the most honest plea Olivia could muster.

With a groan, Cardic pushed Olivia onto her back with more force than either of them had used during this encounter and worked her way down Olivia's body. The feeling of Cardic everywhere, touching her, kissing her as if she needed Olivia's skin to stay alive—it left Olivia awestruck. Finally, Cardic let her fingers drift to the place where Olivia needed them most. Olivia called out, shocked at the sudden fullness and strength of Cardic's fingers. When she thought Cardic's tongue would touch her clit any moment, Cardic crawled back up her body, continuing to work Olivia into a frenzy with her fingers.

Cardic moved to straddle Olivia's thigh and breathed near her ear. The sound of Cardic's breath and the feel of her weight on top of Olivia was even more arousing than the magic of Cardic's fingers. As Olivia clutched Cardic's shoulders in preparation for the explosion, Cardic stopped and looked into her eyes.

"Not yet. With me." Cardic continued the movement of her fingers, which now matched the rhythm of her own hips against Olivia's thigh.

With you.

As Cardic tightened her grip on Olivia's hip and sped up her own thrusts, Olivia let go and crashed over the edge, taking Cardic with her.

The feel of Cardic's soft lips and the gentle kisses against her cheek reminded Olivia of the absurdity of the situation. Olivia didn't do sweet and gentle lovemaking. She didn't look into her lover's eyes as she came. And she certainly never took into account another woman's orgasm when she was worried about her own. Olivia slid from underneath Cardic and stood. Olivia tried and failed to recall a time when she had actually orgasmed at the same time as someone she was sleeping with when it wasn't a ploy to tease her partner and prolong her own pleasure. That was not what this was.

"Olivia," Cardic said from behind her, the covers rustling.

Olivia couldn't look at her. She couldn't look at that beautiful body in her bed. In her home. In her life. No.

Searching for any reason to escape this madness, Olivia almost jumped at the sound of her kitchen timer. *Saved by the bell.*

"Oven's preheated. Take your time getting dressed. I have to get that pie in the oven tonight." Olivia tied the sash of her black silk robe as she walked out of the bedroom, loving and hating the way the smooth material caressed her sensitive nipples. Her body was still damp with sweat and her mouth dry from kissing.

"Olivia." Cardic came out of the bedroom wearing only her jeans, not zipped or buttoned. Like right before the first time they'd made love. Sex. Had sex.

Putting the pie in the oven, Olivia avoided looking anywhere but at Cardic. She tried not to let her name feel like a caress coming from that gorgeous mouth. "Yeah? Hey, if you'd like a beer, I've got a few. Or some milk. I think I'm out of wine."

"Olivia!" Cardic raised her voice the way she had when Olivia had come to her office, the way she probably raised her voice at Clark when he wasn't listening.

Olivia faced Cardic and forced herself to meet her eyes. "What?" She couldn't help the defiant tone in her voice. She probably sounded like Clark when he wasn't listening.

"I love you."

Olivia stared at Cardic, speechless. She opened her mouth but no words came out. Olivia had never had an out-of-body experience, but this was what she imagined it would be like. She watched every millisecond of her relationship with Cardic unfold in front of her eyes. Everything that happened between them, leading to this one point, like dominoes falling in the perfect pattern.

Cardic walked toward Olivia and extended her hand to touch Olivia's shoulder, but Olivia backed up. If Cardic touched her now, she'd agree to anything. She'd fall into those eyes and never come out again. "No."

Pain streaked Cardic's handsome face as she returned her hand to her side after Olivia's rejection of her touch. "I do. I know it's crazy and we didn't plan it, but—"

"You are damn right we didn't plan it. We didn't plan a lot

of what's gone on lately." Olivia gestured toward her bedroom, indicating the fairy-tale encounter from moments before.

"Olivia, don't do this." Cardic's face was a mixture of anguish and dread as she again reached for Olivia.

Olivia attempted to avoid Cardic's eyes, but Cardic bent in front of her and caught her gaze.

"I love you. I know it's insane. It goes against everything I've ever thought I wanted or needed. Shit, it even goes against things as a professional that I disagree with. For me to admit this to you, to anyone...This is real to me, Olivia. I'm in love with you."

Olivia felt sweat bead on her forehead. "No. You need to go. This isn't what we planned. We planned to fuck and now we're done. You need to go." Olivia again backed away from Cardic's touch. Olivia could feel heat moving off her body in waves like the last time she had blood drawn. She prayed for the strength not to pass out. An image of herself in Sleeping Beauty's tower shot through her mind. And being awoken by Prince Charming's kiss. Cardic—the Prince Charming she didn't want or deserve.

Cardic glared at her, and Olivia preferred the anger she saw there to the sad puppy-dog eyes and professions of love.

Olivia turned around and grabbed the edge of the counter, fighting with every fiber of her body the instincts telling her to run toward Cardic and never let her go.

"Please, just go." Olivia's voice was just above a whisper. A tiny whisper was the last defense she had against this woman who had broken every other defense she'd created.

Without another word, Cardic stalked back to the bedroom, grabbed her clothes, and left.

❖

"Auntie, wake up." Clark's small voice penetrated the pleasant haze of sleep Cardic had fallen into. His small chubby hands grabbed Cardic's cheeks.

Cardic pulled Clark toward her chest and tried to gauge the time. "No, let's keep napping."

"No, Auntie, it's time to play. You've been sleeping so long."

Wasn't that the truth. Cardic felt as though she'd been asleep her whole life and only recently woken up to everything that was possible. Love. Family. Even monogamy. But none of that seemed possible without Olivia.

Cardic rubbed her eyes as she sat up on the couch and glanced around her sister's small living room. Claire had an eye for colorful decorating, and Cardic loved her living room. It was cozy with toys and memories everywhere. The worn leather couch with its bounty of embroidered pillows was the perfect place to sleep away her misery.

"Have you called her?" her sister asked.

Cardic was tired of this line of questioning, and she rose from the couch. She held a squealing Clark upside down. After he had begged sufficiently, Cardic set him down and moved toward the kitchen for another beer. "Of course I have. She won't return my calls. Emails. Letters. It's over."

Claire followed her into the kitchen with Clark tagging behind. "There has to be something you can do. Couldn't you just sweep her off—"

"No." Cardic squeezed her eyes shut, praying for patience as she opened another beer. Clark walked up to Cardic and hugged her leg with his warm little arms. She rubbed his shaggy head, suddenly very sad at the thought that she would never even be able to entertain the idea of having kids with Olivia. "She doesn't want this. She doesn't want me. She dug her heels in and that's it. I've gotta move on."

"I understand, Cardic, I really do. I understand heartbreak. But running away to the jungle with Megan isn't the answer."

"You make it sound like a goddamn honeymoon."

Claire looked at Clark then pinned Cardic with a look that meant business. "Language."

Cardic threw her hands up in surrender, wondering what Clark would be like after she missed another year of his life. Cardic exhaled as she ran her hands through her hair and grabbed onto the ends. "I can't be in the same city with her right now. I haven't committed to the entire field study. I told Megan I'd join her until she felt comfortable with the language, then we'll see where things stand." Her guilt almost outweighed her desire to flee. She had been Claire's biggest support system since David all but left the picture, and now her own weakness was pushing her to another continent.

The last two weeks had been torture for Cardic. She'd spent the first week trying to get Olivia at least to speak with her. Vivian, Olivia's assistant, was calm and charming the first fifty times she called, but after that her responses became robotic and less friendly. Olivia wasn't in. For someone who worked sixty or more hours a week, she was sure staying out of the office a lot.

Cardic had no luck with her cell either. At one point, Cardic contemplated leaving a message every time she called Olivia to clog up her voice mail box, knowing the inconvenience would annoy Olivia and get her to at least call back.

Cardic even sank to the ridiculous low of writing love letters. It reminded her of writing notes to girls in her freshman year of high school. She'd shyly sign them *Love, Cardic* and fold them up in interesting shapes, doodling on the margins. No adolescent crush or unrequited teenage lust could compete with the torment of not having Olivia in her life.

Cardic called her cell and her office and sent letters to her apartment, all to no avail. She spent the next seven days trying to distract herself from the constant pain in her gut. Running away to the jungle, as Claire put it, seemed like the perfect option.

"I just don't like seeing you like this."

"Well, I don't like being like this. My entire adult life I've dedicated time and energy to the idea that love is bull—" Cardic hesitated, "poop. And now here I am, head over heels in love with a woman who won't even speak to me. I just need some time to think. To regroup."

Cardic hoped a year in the Amazon would be enough time. Somehow, she doubted it.

❖

"A vacation? But I don't need a vacation." Olivia now argued openly with Mr. McKinnon after the mild suggestion that she take a few weeks off. Olivia attempted to look composed as she brushed the stray hairs away from her face. That morning she'd woken up almost twenty minutes late. Not having time to shower and properly dry her hair, she'd had to improvise an updo. Her unruly curls were reminding her why she didn't attempt to make updos often. What a mess!

"Maybe you don't, but we do." McKinnon pinned her with a look that said he thought her arguing unnecessary because the decision had already been made. "The launch of the new line was incredibly successful, Olivia. You should take time out to enjoy your accomplishments. Plus, I think your team could use some time without you cracking the whip. They all worked hard and need to concentrate on some of the basic day-to-day work to get back into the swing of things. You understand."

No, she didn't understand. Work was life. If she didn't

have work, she didn't have anything. And after throwing Cardic away with both hands, all she'd do on a forced vacation was think about her. Work was the only thing keeping her sanity intact. When thoughts of Cardic threatened, or she avoided one of her calls or threw away one of her letters unopened, all Olivia had to do was jump further into work, letting numbers, budgets, and spreadsheets flood her vision until she could no longer see.

Fine. She'd take a vacation. She could work from home.

"I've also instructed the team that anything you may send for while on vacation is last priority and they can push it back until your return."

Did he think she was cracking up? Did he think her performance was lagging? "Mr. McKinnon, I'm fine. I assure you I—"

"I know you're fine. That's why a vacation will be so enjoyable," he said. "Have Vivian reschedule any meetings you have for the next two weeks. We'll see you then."

The last bit was delivered with finality and a note of authority Olivia wasn't used to hearing from others.

"Thank you, sir." Olivia rose from her chair slowly. Not eating much had been giving her dizzy spells upon standing. There was an apple in her desk. Perhaps she'd eat that before being excommunicated from Vital for the next two weeks.

Back in her office, Olivia sank into her chair and wondered what on earth she could do with herself for two weeks that didn't involve work or reliving every moment she spent with Cardic. What surprised her most was not that she missed sex with Cardic. Olivia knew her body would go through a period of withdrawal after being so thoroughly and consistently pleased. What surprised Olivia was that she missed Cardic. She missed talking with her. She missed their sparing. She missed hearing Cardic talk about the Yanapo.

Olivia tried to shake off the feelings as she took out her cell and called Joan, who picked up on the second ring.

"Can you meet me for an early dinner?"

"Early? As in you're leaving work early? Did the building burn down?"

"Forced vacation."

"Ouch. I'll pick you up at your office at four o'clock. See you then."

Olivia spun around in her chair and stared at the stack of boxes full of samples from the new Vital plus-size line. Gently kicking the top one over with her nude pump, she watched as sports bras and running pants toppled onto the floor in a sea of pastel Lycra.

"Liv, you okay? Just got word from McKinnon about your vacation. Knowing you, I figured it wasn't voluntary." Vivian walked in holding her ever-present yellow legal pad.

"Far from it." Olivia grabbed her purse and took out all the files she usually lugged back and forth from office to home. She powered down her laptop and put it in the top drawer of her desk. "I would tell you to call if you need anything, but I'm sure you've been advised against that." Olivia shrugged and walked toward the door, Vivian still standing in her office.

"Well, I might call you just to check in. I'm sure things will be slow as molasses without you here." Vivian exaggerated her Southern drawl.

"I'm sure they will. Keep everyone afloat. I'll see you in two weeks."

And with that, Olivia left her office for the first vacation she'd taken in her entire career.

It was only three o'clock, so Olivia decided to walk down to the river before Joan picked her up at four. There was a lot of construction going on to improve the river and add sidewalks next to the water with benches and fountains. Most of the construction down the street from Olivia's office was complete, so she descended the steps and walked along the river for a few minutes.

A deep azure sky arched overhead, and there wasn't a cloud in sight. The heavy buildings and skyscrapers cast shadows over the dark blue water. A crowded tour boat floated by the shore, and Olivia thought about the different lives of the many people on board. Where were they going? Who were they? Were they in love?

Olivia sat on a concrete bench flanked by large, leafy plants and removed her sunglasses to study the men and women parading by. A couple walked by hand in hand, looking young and happy. The young man stopped and stared at his companion, gently brushing a strand of hair from her face and pushing it behind her ear. Olivia's insides ached as she thought of the times Cardic looked if she had been tempted to tame her fiery curls. Was that a gesture of affection? Or even love?

Love. What did that word even mean? Olivia wasn't sure, and since the experience had never interested her, she never gave it much thought. Of course she felt love for her father, and it wasn't just the obligatory love of family. Olivia admired him. She strove to be like him in her career, a hardworking leader that never gave up. She also admired his outlook on life. It could not have been easy raising a rambunctious child like her, especially alone.

But his outlook on love was something she didn't share. He seemed to chase after it with a deep sense of urgency as if love was a rainbow after a storm, one that would disappear if he didn't find the pot of gold at the end.

"Olivia? Olivia Reynolds?"

Olivia looked up toward a weary voice addressing her. She couldn't place the owner of the voice. "Yes? May I help you?" As big as Chicago was, it wasn't unheard of to run into a coworker or acquaintance, and Olivia took pride that her networking abilities made it happen fairly often.

The woman was petite and non-threatening. She took off her sunglasses and held out her hand. Her fingers were warm and slender, her handshake firm. There was something familiar about the woman, but Olivia couldn't place her.

"I'm sure you don't remember me. I'm Laura Stills. My husband was—"

"Adam. Of course." Olivia and Adam had kept in touch briefly after college but lost touch soon after. She'd met his young wife at their fifteen-year high school reunion. "I'm terribly sorry for your loss. Adam was such a great man."

"Yes, he was. And thank you for the lovely flowers. They meant a lot to me."

"It was the least I could do." Olivia shuddered. It really was the least she could do. She should have attended his funeral. She should have called Laura. She should have been a friend to Adam and actually stayed in touch.

"You and Adam had such a competitive relationship. He spoke of your drive and passion often," Laura said as she wiped a stray tear from her eye. It hadn't been long since the death of her husband. How did a person even begin to get over the complete loss of someone they loved?

Suddenly, Olivia's stomach dropped. She realized with certainty that there was comfort in the fact that Cardic was off somewhere teaching, reading, breathing. The idea that Cardic was alive and well somewhere, even without her, gave her a measure of comfort that Laura was no longer afforded. She'd loved Adam and given him everything she could, and now he was gone. Olivia glanced down at Laura's hand. She wore a small solitaire diamond ring and her wedding band. Laura gently twisted the band with her finger.

Cardic was still here, on this earth, and Olivia had pushed her away.

Olivia's mind shot to the future, she and Joan sitting in some bar having the same conversations about the same meaningless work garbage, and Joan sliding Cardic's obituary toward her on the bar table. Her throat constricted, and Olivia glanced back at the bench she had vacated when Laura approached her.

"I'm sorry, I just need…"

"Whoa, are you okay? Here, sit down. Would you like some water?" Olivia was amazed at how quickly Laura went from teary widow to Good Samaritan. Olivia searched Laura's red-rimmed eyes and realized she must just walk around in a constant state of grief. Tears rolled down Olivia's cheeks, much to her embarrassment. She attempted the breathing technique her therapist had taught her in tenth grade. *In: one, two, three, four. Out: one, two, three, four.* As Olivia's vision returned to normal, she glanced at Laura, realizing she'd shown more emotion to this near stranger than she had to Joan in nearly a decade.

"I'm so sorry, Laura. I've just got a lot on my mind. And I wish I could have been there for you and Adam."

"Oh, nonsense. He knew he had your support, even if you weren't nearby." Laura waved a hand as she pulled a small packet of tissues from her purse.

Did Cardic know? Did Cardic know she had Olivia's support even if she wasn't there? She wasn't there because she was a coward and she was too stubborn and too much of a control freak to admit what Cardic was observant enough to see.

I have to see her. I have to tell her.

"I'm so sorry, Laura, but I've really got to be going." She

handed Laura one of her business cards, then wrapped her in a hug. "Please, call me. I'd like to take you to dinner. We could talk. Catch up." Olivia was surprised at her offer but knew the moment she said it that she had meant it.

Olivia hurried toward LaSalle Street and hailed a cab, calling Joan on the way to cancel their plans.

Olivia just hoped Cardic would see her.

Chapter Twenty-Two

Cardic nursed her third beer as Megan droned on about flights, layovers, bug spray, and notepads. Cardic would have to go through her pack and find her original list of "must-haves." She still hadn't unpacked her pack from her return. Something about it still being full and ready to go in her closet made her feel closer to her tribe. She'd need more of those stretchy bug repellant bracelets.

"Cardic? Cardic, are you even listening?" Megan arched a delicate blond eyebrow and came to sit on the couch next to Cardic.

"Yeah, no, I'm listening." Cardic sat a little straighter to see if it would make her appear more interested. The more she thought about leaving the U.S. for a year, the more she just wanted to go. To hell with the planning. She rubbed her tired eyes and was surprised to feel Megan's hand on her thigh.

"I think this is such a great opportunity for us. I'm so glad you agreed."

Cardic looked at Megan's face. She was beautiful in the plainest sense of the word. A straight nose, bright blue eyes, and thick straight blond hair. She was about Cardic's height but slightly more curvaceous. Gone was the skinny college girl Cardic had once spent so much time with. Sitting in front of her now, rubbing her hand up and down Cardic's thigh, sat an eligible, successful, and sexy woman. And Cardic felt nothing. Nothing but annoyance.

If this feeling wasn't monogamy, Cardic didn't know what was.

Cardic closed her eyes and prayed for the rush of warmth that usually came when a willing woman was nearby. She concentrated on the feel of Megan's hand on her thigh, but her nails were long, and they made a scratching sound on her jeans. She tried to concentrate on the smell of Megan's perfume, but it was too sweet and almost made her nauseous.

Cardic pried Megan's wandering hand off her leg and turned to look at her. "Megan, I'm flattered that you included me in this work opportunity. But that's all this is to me—work. It's great to see you, and we've talked about some great times tonight, but that's all it is."

"I know you're not the relationship type anymore, Cardic. I get that." She scooted closer until her leg draped lazily nearby. Megan rubbed the nape of Cardic's neck, those long nails digging into her skin. "But I'm not talking about a relationship. I'm talking about working during working hours, and anything we want during off hours."

Cardic couldn't help the skin-crawling feeling that consumed her at receiving Megan's touch. She didn't want to hurt her or embarrass her, but this shit was so not going to happen.

"Megan." Cardic stood and began to pace. "Again, I'm very flattered, but I'm not interested in an affair either."

"Why not? Are you with someone?" Megan's face turned to a grin as she appeared to hold back a laugh.

Cardic straightened her back and shoved her hands into her pockets, her irritation quickly turning to anger. "Not that it's any of your business, but no, I'm not."

"Then what's the problem? Our relationship was a disaster, I'll give you that, but come on, Cardic, it was the best sex."

Until Olivia.

"I'm sorry, Megan, I'm not going to bend on this. The only way I will continue to entertain the idea of joining you on this study is if you agree, right now, that's all it is."

Before Megan could answer, a knock sounded at Cardic's door. Cicero left the comfort of his bed for the first time that evening and trotted over with excitement.

Cardic stared at Megan for a moment, waiting for her answer. Megan stared right back and didn't say a word.

When the knock sounded again, a little more insistent, Cardic walked toward the door, ignoring Megan's huff of annoyance.

Cardic pulled open the door, kicking Cicero back with her leg, and almost fell over as she stared into the green eyes that had haunted her for over two weeks. Olivia looked like she'd just come from work, her bag hefted on her shoulder, wearing a dark red skirt and a black top.

"Olivia," Cardic breathed, only because she was too shocked to use her voice.

"Hi." Olivia glanced at Cardic, and a hesitant smile appeared on her lips.

Cardic thought that was a good sign until Olivia's eyes darted past her and Cicero and landed on Megan.

"I'm sorry, you're busy. I should have called. I just... I'm sorry." Olivia backed away and backed right up into the hallway wall, dropping her bag.

Cardic rushed to her side, picking up her bag and touching her at the elbow. "Don't go. This is work. Come in." Cardic again had trouble finding her voice. Looking into Olivia's eyes, she pleaded for her to stay, just for a minute. An hour. Forever.

Olivia nodded once and walked into Cardic's apartment as if she had every right to be there. She sat on a worn leather chair and crossed her legs. Now, those were legs, not those dinky things Megan had brought with her. Olivia sat upright, spine straight, with poise and confidence and looked Megan right in the face. If Cardic were the optimistic type, she would have thought the look almost predatory.

"Megan, this is Olivia. Olivia, Megan. A colleague." Cardic gestured between them and walked to the coffee table, packing up Megan's things in her bag without even asking. "Megan, let me walk you out. We can finish this next week."

Megan glanced between Cardic and Olivia with a puzzled expression, then reluctantly took her bag from Cardic and headed toward the door. "Well, I'll send you the itinerary I come up with."

"And we're clear on everything else?" Cardic held the door open for Megan and pinned her with a stare, indicating their earlier conversation. Cardic resisted the overwhelming urge to physically push her out the door.

Megan looked from Cardic to Olivia, then back again, seeming to put the pieces together. Looking irritated and disappointed, Megan answered, "Yes. I understand."

As the gorgeous blonde departed, Olivia felt herself relax a little. It wasn't within the terms of their sexual arrangement or her recent treatment of Cardic for her to ask questions or stake claims. But it had taken everything in her not to crawl onto Cardic's back and howl at the other woman like a wild animal. She knew the look on that woman's face. Megan. Whoever she was. She wanted Cardic. Badly. Like any woman in her right mind would.

"Megan is a colleague." Cardic closed the door after Megan left and leaned against it, almost as if she was too weary to approach Olivia, but also blocking the exit in case she tried to leave.

"Itinerary? Are you going somewhere?"

"Back to the Amazon."

Olivia stared. *I've lost her. I blew it.* "The Amazon. Wow. Well, I know you wanted to go back. I'm sorry. It's really none of my business."

"Yes, it is."

"Why?"

"You know why."

Olivia couldn't look into those eyes any longer. It felt as if every secret she'd ever had sank into the depths of those deep brown eyes. Like nothing belonged to her anymore, not her body, not her thoughts. Not her heart.

"When you said what you said before…" Olivia stopped, not knowing how to continue.

"That I'm in love with you?" Cardic moved a few steps closer.

"Yes. That." Olivia cleared her throat and stood, twisting her hands together to keep from grabbing Cardic by the arms and screaming for her not to leave.

Olivia dealt with consequences of her actions and took responsibility. If Cardic was about to head back to the jungle with Malibu Barbie, then she'd deal with it. But not before saying what she needed to say.

"I didn't know how to respond or what to say. All I knew is that I was scared. Scared of losing even more control than I already had. Scared of not knowing when or how things would end. Just scared of so many things."

"Olivia." Cardic again stepped closer to her, but this time Olivia stood her ground.

"No, please let me get this out. When I'm with you, it's

like I'm not myself. At least not the self I've worked so hard to create. And I don't know how to be this person sometimes."

"I'm not trying to pressure you."

Cardic seemed concerned that she'd done something wrong. Olivia's heart broke a little more.

"But I realized something today. Even when I told you to leave, it's like I knew you'd still be there. Somewhere. But I don't want to take that for granted. I don't want to be complacent in the idea that you are just existing somewhere. I want..." Olivia stopped speaking altogether as tears threatened.

Cardic closed the distance between them and cupped Olivia's face in her warm, strong hands. "You want what?" Cardic stared into those green eyes, waiting, praying to hear something from Olivia's lips that would ease the decaying of her insides.

"I want to exist with you. I want to be with you whenever I can. I'm tired of trysts and quick fucks. I want to sleep with you and wake up with you in the morning. I want you to have a say in what happens, not just in the bedroom. Everywhere."

Cardic closed her eyes and rested her forehead against Olivia's, wondering what happened to her life. The safe, compartmentalized, orderly life she had led only months ago. And she didn't care. She didn't want that life. Cardic wanted a life with Olivia.

"But you're leaving. You're going back to the tribe."

Before Olivia could even finish her thought, Cardic took her mouth in a kiss, a kiss that Olivia felt everywhere, inside and out.

"No, no. I'm not going anywhere."

"But Megan and the field—"

Cardic cut her off again with more kisses and nips at her lips as she backed Olivia toward her bedroom, "No, I don't care. I'm not leaving this city. And you aren't leaving my bed until I say." Cardic grinned, looking more like herself since Olivia had walked in the door.

Grabbing Olivia's ass, Cardic attacked her neck and tossed her on the bed, lying on top of her and letting her full weight rest against Olivia's body.

"Yes." Olivia closed her eyes and let a feeling of completeness and happiness wash over her as she surrendered to the hands of her lover, knowing any life with Cardic would surpass even the most extravagant fantasies of a life without her.

EPILOGUE

"Honey, I'm home," Cardic shouted as she walked into Olivia's apartment and set her books and bag down next to the entry table.

"You're so lame." Olivia laughed from her comfy spot on the couch. In the last week of her forced vacation, Cardic introduced her to a fiction series, and she was about to finish the last one before her return to work on Monday. Cardic had never seen Olivia look so relaxed. "How did it go?"

Cardic plopped down on the couch and rested her head in Olivia's lap. During their affair, she'd had many impulses to do such intimate and mundane things, but she'd never indulged herself. Now that they had agreed to "see where things went," she was indulging in every single ridiculous thing she could think of. Holding hands walking down the street. Sleeping in on the weekends. Tickling Olivia while brushing their teeth.

"Of course Davenport wasn't too receptive, but the president and head of curriculum thought the new class would be a perfect fit."

Since Cardic would no longer be joining Megan on her field study, she needed to think fast about how to save her job. In light of her new lease on life, she decided to propose a new graduate-level course.

"Great," Olivia said as she put down her book and unbuttoned Cardic's shirt.

"Mm-hmm. So as of this fall, you are looking at the professor of the new anthropology five hundred course: Marriage and Kinship."

Olivia's wandering hands made it hard to think, but Cardic was tired of thinking. Her life had been spent organizing, cataloging, and analyzing data. Enough thinking. It was about time she experienced something different. Cardic yearned to experience what she had only observed in others—lasting love.

About the Author

Jane Hardee lives in Chicago, Illinois, with her partner, two dogs, and a cat. She is a special education teacher who loves going to work every day with a passion for autism.

Instagram: @janehardee
Email: janehardee4@gmail.com.

Books Available From Bold Strokes Books

A Heart to Call Home by Jeannie Levig. When Jessie Weldon returns to her hometown after thirty years, can she and her childhood crush Dakota Scott heal the tragic past that links them? (978-1-63555-059-7)

Children of the Healer by Barbara Ann Wright. Life becomes desperate for ex-soldier Cordelia Ross when the indigenous aliens of her planet are drawn into a civil war and old enemies linger in the shadows. Book Three of the Godfall Series. (978-1-63555-031-3)

Hearts Like Hers by Melissa Brayden. Coffee shop owner Autumn Primm is ready to cut loose and live a little, but is the baggage that comes with out-of-towner Kate Carpenter too heavy for anything long term? (978-1-63555-014-6)

Love at Cooper's Creek by Missouri Vaun. Shaw Daily flees corporate life to find solace in the rural Blue Ridge Mountains, but escapism eludes her when her attentions are captured by small town beauty Kate Elkins. (978-1-62639-960-0)

Twice in a Lifetime by PJ Trebelhorn. Detective Callie Burke can't deny the growing attraction to her late friend's widow, Taylor Fletcher, who also happens to own the bar where Callie's sister works. (978-1-63555-033-7)

Undiscovered Affinity by Jane Hardee. Will a no-strings-attached affair be enough to break Olivia's control and convince Cardic that love does exist? (978-1-63555-061-0)

Between Sand and Stardust by Tina Michele. Are the lifelong bonds of love strong enough to conquer time, distance, and heartache when Haven Thorne and Willa Bennette are given another chance at forever? (978-1-62639-940-2)

Charming the Vicar by Jenny Frame. When magician and atheist Finn Kane seeks refuge in an English village after a spiritual crisis, can local vicar Bridget Claremont restore her faith in life and love? (978-1-63555-029-0)

Data Capture by Jesse J. Thoma. Lola Walker is undercover on the hunt for cybercriminals while trying not to notice the woman who might be perfectly wrong for her for all the right reasons. (978-1-62639-985-3)

Epicurean Delights by Renee Roman. Ariana Marks had no idea a leisure swim would lead to being rescued, in more ways than one, by the charismatic Hudson Frost. (978-1-63555-100-6)

Heart of the Devil by Ali Vali. We know most of Cain and Emma Casey's story, but Heart of the Devil will take you back to where it began one fateful night with a tray loaded with beer. (978-1-63555-045-0)

Known Threat by Kara A. McLeod. When Special Agent Ryan O'Connor reluctantly questions who protects the Secret Service, she learns courage truly is found in unlikely places. Agent O'Connor Series #3 (978-1-63555-132-7)

Seer and the Shield by D. Jackson Leigh. Time is running out for the Dragon Horse Army while two unlikely heroines struggle to put aside their attraction and find a way to stop a deadly cult. Dragon Horse War, Book 3 (978-1-63555-170-9)

The Universe Between Us by Jane C. Esther. Ana Mitchell must make the hardest choice of her life: the promise of new love Jolie Dann on Earth, or a humanity-saving mission to colonize Mars. (978-1-63555-106-8)

Touch by Kris Bryant. Can one touch heal a heart? (978-1-63555-084-9)

A More Perfect Union by Carsen Taite. Major Zoey Granger and DC fixer Rook Daniels risk their reputations for a chance at true love while dealing with a scandal that threatens to rock the military. (978-1-62639-754-5)

Arrival by Gun Brooke. The spaceship *Pathfinder* reaches its passengers' new homeworld where danger lurks in the shadows while Pamas Seclan disembarks and finds unexpected love in young science genius Darmiya Do Voy. (978-1-62639-859-7)

Captain's Choice by VK Powell. Architect Kerstin Anthony's life is going to plan until Bennett Carlyle, the first girl she ever kissed, is assigned to her latest and most important project, a police district substation. (978-1-62639-997-6)

Falling Into Her by Erin Zak. Pam Phillips, widow at the age of forty, meets Kathryn Hawthorne, local Chicago celebrity, and it changes her life forever—in ways she hadn't even considered possible. (978-1-63555-092-4)

Hookin' Up by MJ Williamz. Will Leah get what she needs from casual hookups or will she see the love she desires right in front of her? (978-1-63555-051-1)

King of Thieves by Shea Godfrey. When art thief Casey Marinos meets bounty hunter Finnegan Starkweather, the crimes of the past just might set the stage for a payoff worth more than she ever dreamed possible. (978-1-63555-007-8)

Lucy's Chance by Jackie D. As a serial killer haunts the streets, Lucy tries to stitch up old wounds with her first love in the wake of a small town's rapid descent into chaos. (978-1-63555-027-6)

Right Here, Right Now by Georgia Beers. When Alicia Wright moves into the office next door to Lacey Chamberlain's accounting firm, Lacey is about to find out that sometimes the last person you want is exactly the person you need. (978-1-63555-154-9)

Strictly Need to Know by MB Austin. Covert operator Maji Rios will do whatever she must to complete her mission, but saving a gorgeous stranger from Russian mobsters was not in her plans. (978-1-63555-114-3)

Tailor-Made by Yolanda Wallace. Tailor Grace Henderson doesn't date clients, but when she meets gender-bending model Dakota Lane, she's tempted to throw all the rules out the window. (978-1-63555-081-8)

Time Will Tell by M. Ullrich. With the ability to time travel, Eva Caldwell will have to decide between having it all and erasing it all. (978-1-63555-088-7)